# HALLO-TWEEN

Lisa Nardini
Gina Nardini
Sucia Nardini
Marina Ummel

Cover Art:
Gina Nardini

**Sorelle Publishing Inc.**

Copyright © 2012 Sorelle Publishing Inc.

All rights reserved.

No part of this book may be reproduced, scanned, or distributed in any printed or electronic form without permission.

*This book is dedicated to anyone who has told a scary story on a dark autumn night.*

# CONTENTS

Acknowledgments

# ACKNOWLEDGMENTS

The Nardini Sisters would like to thank their editor, Lou Belcher, for her insightful assistance. They would also like to thank Jessica Lowell, for additional editing. Mary Nardini, (mom) and Renae get kudos for reading our rough draft and giving valued feedback.

Lisa would like to thank Sparky, who lives in the timber!

Gina would like to thank her husband Scott. She would also like to thank her students for allowing her to tell a scary story every once and a while.

Sucia: I would like to thank my sisters for giving me a chance to write, and my mom and brothers for always being there. I would also like to thank my son, Josh, who is proudly serving as a Marine, and my talented and beautiful daughter, Marina. And to my hus-band Chris, never stop singing to me!

Marina: I would like to thank my mom and dad for their continued support and love.

.

# RADIO

**It** was a cool Saturday in October and I had just spent the day with my Grandpa at the local farmer's market selling pumpkins. He let me drive his old battered pick-up truck home even though I'd only had my license a short time. We talked about the day and life's small things as we watched the long country miles pass by. When we got home, Grandma had a light supper ready, so we washed up and dug in.

"Are you sure you don't mind me borrowing the old pick-up tonight?" I asked for the millionth time. Even though I was spending the weekend with my grandparents, I had made plans to meet some of my friends in town. We were going to see the latest scary movie and hopefully run into some pretty girls, too.

"I don't mind, but you know you can take the sedan," Grandpa said. "It's in much better shape."

"No, I'm okay with the truck," I said and I really was. I loved the old truck. Heck, I remember riding in it around the farm when I was just a boy. I would sit on Grandpa's lap and help him steer while the radio blared the latest country song.

"Okay Sport, just be safe," he said.

Later that night, after I'd showered and dressed, I said goodnight to my grandparents and headed out. The old truck rattled and shook as she ate up the country miles. It was dusk when I got to town to meet my friends. We caught a scary movie, flirted with a few girls, and ate some fast food. It was getting close to midnight, so I decided to head on home, knowing I had a long drive ahead of me.

The night had turned a bit foggy. I drove slowly to make sure I didn't hit anything. It wasn't uncommon for a deer to leap out on the road unexpectedly.

I decided to listen to some music to keep me company. When I turned on the radio, a talk show came on. It was one I had never heard before called, *The Sandman Forum*.

The topic of discussion was true-life paranormal stories. It sounded intriguing so I decided to listen.

An older gentleman with a thick country accent was telling a story to the host: *"When I was a young man, I was driving home late one night on a deserted country road. It was foggy and I was driving slowly to make sure I didn't hit any little critters who were trying to cross the road."*

*"Kinda like tonight,"* the announcer said interrupting the old man.

*"Exactly like tonight,"* the old man said.

Creepy, I thought and shivered a little.

*"Anyway, I'd been driving just a little bit when I saw some movement on the side of the road. I braked slightly because I thought it was a deer."*

Just as the old man paused in his story, I caught a movement out of the corner of my eye. It flashed by the passenger side of the truck like a black streak. I shook my head. I was just paranoid. Surely, it was just the suggestion of the old man's story making me see things that weren't there.

*"So, was it a deer?"* the announcer asked.

*"No, course not. I wouldn't call into your show for a deer sighting now would I? No*

*sir, it was something much more sinister than that."*

*"A bear?"*

*"I'm afraid to say, but it was not of this world."*

*At that, the announcer chuckled and said, "Come on, now. You can't have us believe it was some spook or specter?"*

*"Let me finish the story and then you can be the judge."*

*"Fair enough."*

*"I drove another mile or so. I was barely down to a crawl because the fog was so thick."*

Just as the old man finished saying this, it was as if I hit a wall of fog. I slammed on the brakes and slowed down to a crawl myself. I wasn't feeling too comfortable with the similarities between his story and my current situation. I laughed nervously. I told myself to get a grip. I was a pretty big guy and wasn't one to get frightened easily. I had never been afraid of the dark or walked away from a fight. I could hold my own, I reminded myself.

*The old man continued, "I was coming to a narrow section in the road that was overgrown with trees."*

4

I listened spellbound before I realized that I too was entering into an area where the road narrowed and the tree canopy overlapped. I was beginning to wonder if the old man was talking about this very stretch of road I was on. I usually like driving down this road. It was really pretty in the daytime. The trees branches intertwined creating a natural tunnel; when you drove in, the hot summer air cooled by ten degrees. But at night it was really scary, like the tree tops became finger tips that enveloped you.

*"Everything was fine until I got about halfway through,"* the old man said.

*"Hang on to that thought, we need to take a station break,"* the announcer said.

I gripped the wheel tightly as I listened to the commercials. I took a deep breath and tried to relax. I was being silly. There wasn't anything to worry about. I started whistling along with one of the commercial jingles, but stopped short when I saw two red eyes peering at me from a low hanging branch. At the same time, something scurried across the road in front of me.

I slammed on the brakes so as not to hit whatever it was that decided to cross the road. Thankfully I missed it, but could have sworn I heard a thump of something falling into the bed of the pickup truck. Oddly, the thump came as I drove under the low hanging branch with the red-eyed mystery creature.

I knew I should look back at the truck bed to see what it was, but I was just too scared.

*"Welcome back to The Sandman Forum,"* the announcer said, *"We are talking about true paranormal stories and had to take a break, but we're back and ready to hear the rest. Caller, please continue."*

*"As I drove under those trees, I spied an odd sight. Two red-eyes peered at me from a low hanging branch,"* the old man said, *"I'm pretty sure whatever it was jumped on-to the roof of my car."*

No! How could this be? Just then I heard a scratching sound coming from the bed of my truck. It was probably a raccoon, I told my-self.

*"How'd you know it was on your roof?"* the announcer asked.

*"I heard scratching. I knew in my soul it was something evil,"* the old man said.

*"So what did you do?"* the announcer asked.

*"I remembered my Sunday School teach-*

*ing, is what,"* he said.

*"What does that mean?"*

Yeah, what did that mean? This was silly. I was probably riding around with a cute little baby possum that fell out of the tree. I had to know. I willed myself to look in the rearview mirror to make sure nothing sinister was riding with me. I told myself I would look on the count of three. One, two…

*"Don't look at it!"* the old man screamed as if his message was meant just for me.

I was really scared. I jerked the wheel and heard something roll around in the bed of the truck.

*"That was your Sunday School lesson?"* the announcer asked.

*"Yes sir. We were taught to not look upon the face of evil. And I didn't."*

As he said this, it was as if my eyes could not help but wander up to the rearview mirror. A moment before, I didn't want to look; now I couldn't help myself. I willed myself to keep my eyes on the road even though the scratching got louder.

*"I'm telling you, that evil will try everything to get you to notice it. Because next came the wailing,"* he said.

Just as he said that, I heard a loud screech.

I could barely hold onto the wheel and my breaths were coming in short bursts. I swear couldn't recall a time I had been this scared. The wailing continued. I turned up the radio to drown it out and to listen to the guest speaker. Maybe his advice could help me.

*"If I live to a hundred, I will never forget that wailing. It bore right into my soul. I knew if I looked at the evil creature I would be turned to stone or something just as biblical,"* the old man said.

I didn't want to be turned to stone, so I decided right then and there not to look at it. The wailing suddenly stopped.

*"The wailing stopped as quickly as it started. I felt a moment's relief until I heard the growling noise. It was worse than the wailing, if that was possible. And it wasn't coming from the hood; it was coming from under my car. Had I run over something that was still hanging on to the tires?"* the caller asked.

I too felt some relief as I didn't hear any growling noise. The fog instantly turned so thick I couldn't see two feet in front of me. I slowed down a bit, but felt the car shudder as if I hit something in the road. I didn't stop driving. The fog dissipated and I could hear a faint murmuring. I rolled down my window and immediately wished I hadn't. It was not a murmur I was hearing, it was growling; and it was coming from under my car.

*"What did you do?" the announcer asked.*

I was waiting for the answer also.

*"I did what every God-fearing southern man would do: I started praying. Praying loudly," he said.*

*"Did it work?" the announcer asked.*

*"It most certainly did not, which made me realize that what was happening must be supernatural. I pulled over and armed myself with the only things I could think of: my trusty Swiss Army knife and my flashlight.*

I felt in my pants pocket; I had the Swiss Army knife that my grandpa had given me. I pulled it out. I also opened the glove compartment and retrieved the flashlight. Did I have the guts to pull over like the caller? I wasn't sure.

*"So, I was standing outside with my knife pointed at the darkness, when I saw the most unbelievable sight I could have ever imaged. It was as if I was in a monster movie. I turned the flashlight on the scene before me, and jumped back in my truck," the caller*

*said as the radio turned to static.*

I banked the car to the side of the road and stepped out with my knife. I don't know where I got the courage. The growling continued. Suddenly, a shadow leapt from under the truck. The creature in the back flew down upon the shadow. In a flash, they were inter-twined in a scuffle. I don't think they even saw me. I stepped back and aimed the flashlight on them. What I saw sent chills down my spine. The red-eyed creature was a pale vampire and the growling creature was a werewolf!

They were locked into a fight to the death. I tried to quickly scramble into the car without letting them see me, but I slipped on some loose gravel causing them to momentarily stop fighting. When they realized I had seen them, the vampire turned into a bat and flew over my head and the werewolf loped off into the woods. I jumped into the car, locked the doors and pushed down the accelerator as far as it would go. I took off and never looked back. I was sweating and had chills at the same time.

The radio was on, but it was still just static. That was okay because I was pretty sure I knew what the old caller had seen. I turned the radio off and drove the rest of the way home in silence.

When I entered my grandpa's house, I handed him the keys. All I wanted to do was sleep.

"Did the truck run okay for you tonight?" Grandpa asked before I headed upstairs.

"Yeah, thanks again. I probably won't need it the rest of the week." I told him. I was pretty sure I wasn't going back on those roads again.

"Yep, she's a good truck. Only bad thing is that the radio has been busted for a long time now. I keep meaning to get it fixed but never get around to it," he said.

"No, grandpa, the radio works fine. I listened to it tonight," I told him.

"Not possible. The antenna broke several years ago."

The hairs on the back of my neck stood up straight. There was no way I was getting any sleep tonight.

# CHARMED

**I** knew I wasn't pretty, but I also knew I wasn't ugly. I just knew I was unusual. I answer to Raven, and my hair is wild and very dark. Midnight was the word I heard the most when describing my locks. My eyes are green, but they aren't normal. My pupils are diagonally slanted, just like a cat. People whisper about my looks all the time.

Even with all this, I had a small circle of friends who I trusted.

I did not have the lights turned on this All Hallow's Eve, because the moon was so full and red that a beam of light shone through my attic window. Yes, my room was in the attic. I begged my parents to let me move up there. They didn't want me to, but relented when I said it was all I wanted for my twelfth birthday.

That was six months ago. My friends and I had so much fun decorating it. Ruby, who has flaming red hair, painted one wall red, of course. It was the wall that my bed was up against. I had the prettiest black comforter on my bed. The contrast between the wall and the bed was fantastic! Pearl has hair so light that it is almost white. She painted my dresser white and all the shelves above it white, too. I'm not sure what color Prism's hair is because every month she changes the color. This month it was purple. Since Prism loved different colors, she painted a huge rainbow that arched across the wall over my attic window. I liked it. It made me happy.

While sitting by my window, I caught a glimpse from the corner of my eye. It was a figure hiding behind the large oak tree in our front yard. Our front yard had three small trees surrounding the large oak. I decided to go down and investigate. This particular time of year was ripe for pranks.

"Throw me a roll!" the big boy known as Bubba said. A roll of toilet paper went sailing and, to his credit, Bubba caught it as if it were a football.

"Nice catch," Nate said. He was slighter

than Bubba in height and in build.

"This is going to take all night. That oak tree is gigantic. Maybe we should just toilet paper that tree and forget about the others," Denny suggested. He was Bubba's younger brother, and would one day be just as big.

"I dunno, maybe." Bubba said as he expertly slung the roll around a high branch.

Nate didn't have the strength in his upper body to throw the rolls of toilet paper into the big tree, so he decided to tackle the smaller trees. "Hey, I could probably get this done in ten minutes." He bragged.

"Good, because that's probably all the time we have left before someone spies us," Denny said.

"I don't think anyone's home tonight. Raven's parents are at the big party downtown, the same one my parents go to every year," Nate said.

"How do you know that?" Bubba asked.

"My parents told me that Raven's parents were hired out to read tarot cards, and to tell fortunes and true-life ghost stories. It kinda sounded fun. I wish I could have gone, but it was just for adults."

"Maybe Raven's home," Denny said.

"Naw, there weren't any lights on in the

house. She's a little weird, but I don't think she'd sit by herself in a dark house all night, especially on Halloween," Nate explained.

Just then, a black cat jumped down from the oak tree and landed right in the middle of the boys. They all jumped back and looked at each other. A stiff wind blew between them. The cat let out a couple of very loud meows, and that was more than enough to send the boys running.

They regrouped at the end of the block.

"That was weird," Bubba said.

"Yeah, it was as if that cat was really mad at us for toilet papering the house," Nate said.

"Why would a cat care if we did that? It's just a cat," Denny said.

"Yeah, but it's Raven's cat. Maybe it has special powers. Who knows?" Bubba said.

"That's ridiculous. Let's go back and finish the job. We were almost done," Nate said.

As the boys made their way back towards Raven's house, they ran across a white cat. The cat arched its back and hissed at them. They zipped up their jackets as a cold wind blew by them.

"What's with all the cats tonight?" Denny

asked.

"I dunno, it's spooky. I'm more of a dog person myself," Bubba said.

"Yeah, me too. Gimme a dog over a cat any day," Nate said and laughed.

The boys stood frozen on the street in front of Raven's house. They could not believe their eyes. The trees were totally bare, not one swatch of toilet paper anywhere. The wind was getting stronger.

"How could that be?" Nate whispered.

"We weren't gone that long," Denny said.

"Maybe the wind blew all the toilet paper away," Bubba said.

They all nodded, but they knew it wasn't true.

"I guess we go with plan B," Nate said. "Let's meet back here in a half hour with supplies."

This time the nods were only half-hearted.

A multi-colored tabby cat weaved its way through Bubba's legs, causing him to jump and scream.

"Oh my gosh! This town is outta control with cats. Scat!" He kicked it hard. The tabby hissed and raced away.

"That's teaching it!" Denny said.

**Raven** checked out the boy's toilet paper

prank. "Amateurs," she laughed. She was back in the attic and had decided to call her friends over. She had a feeling the boys would be back and that the pranks were going to go on all night. She might as well have a little fun with them too. And she knew her girlfriends would want to be a part of it.

The girls got there fast. They were all huddled in the attic watching from the window.

"Do you really think they'll come back?" Prism asked, as she rubbed a fresh bruise on her arm.

"Definitely. Those boys aren't the sharpest tools in the shed," Pearl said, laughing.

"Let's make some popcorn. This might be a long night," Ruby suggested.

We brought the popcorn and sodas back up to the attic. We kept the lights off so the boys would think that no one was home.

"What do you think they will do next?" Pearl asked.

"I would bet rotten eggs or throwing eggs. Something to do with eggs. These guys are quite predictable," I said with a mouth full of popcorn.

And just as I finished my sentence, we

heard the SPLAT of an egg hitting the mailbox.

"You were right. They are very predicttable," Prism laughed.

Ruby excused herself to go to the bathroom.

"Grab some more sodas!" I yelled to her.

"And a milk!" Pearl added.

"No problem!" Ruby yelled back.

**"Nice** throw," Denny said to Bubba.

"Yeah, maybe I should be on the baseball team too," Bubba said proudly.

"I want to smash one on their door," Nate said.

"Why would you want to get that close? They say this house is haunted," Denny said.

"Duh, why else would we be here?" Nate said. "I'm going up." Armed with an egg in each hand, Nate walked toward the front door with long strides.

As Nate got closer, his stride got shorter.

"He's getting scared," Bubba said.

"Wouldn't you?" Denny asked.

"Oh yeah. I wouldn't do it at all. I don't know if we should even be standing here," Bubba said looking around, even though there wasn't a soul in sight.

"He's stopping," Denny said.

And true enough, Nate stopped about five feet shy of the front door. He was about to throw an egg, when out of nowhere a cat jumped on his back. Nate was so frightened that he dropped the eggs and ran back to the other boys.

"What in the devil was that?" Nate asked in a shaky voice.

"It was another cat; a red cat," Denny said.

"Did you say a red cat?" Nate asked.

"Yep, red alright. It ran by here after it jumped on you," Bubba said.

Still shaken up, Nate declared, "I think I'm done here. Can we leave now?"

Bubba said, "I've been ready all night."

"Let's go," Denny said.

The boys walked away from the house and headed home.

**What** did I miss?" Ruby asked, coming upstairs with our drinks.

"Victory is ours," Pearl exclaimed.

"Not so fast," I said.

"What did you have in mind?" Prism asked.

"Maybe a taste of their own medicine,

perhaps?" I said.

"Should I get the spell book or the curses book?" Ruby asked.

Pearl reached over and plucked something out of Ruby's hair.

"Ewww. What was it?" Ruby asked.

"I don't know? Eggshell?" Pearl said, and we all laughed.

Prism placed the spell book in the middle of my bedroom. Ruby placed the saucer of milk next to the book.

"Places, ladies," I said.

I snapped my fingers first, then Ruby, then Pearl and finally Prism. We withdrew to our respectable places in order for the spell to work.

I lay on my bed blending in with my comforter, licking my paws. Ruby was scratching her back against the red wall; she blended in so easy I could barely see her. Pearl was playing on a white shelf, and all I could see were her eyes. Prism was walking across the top of the window; her tabby coat blending in with the different colors.

Down the street, three scruffy dogs padded home where three boys once stood. The spell was complete.

# GREED

**I'm** pretty sure my parents are aliens. I know this because they actually said I could go out with my friends tonight unsupervised. They said it was because I was a teenager now. Halloween night and no parents tagging along? Sweet!

My friends and I decided to meet at the end of the block by the school. We all agreed our costumes had to be scary and we also agreed not to tell each other what we were going to be. Mine was so awesome. I rummaged through our junk closet and came up with a rainbow wig, an old red coat, and a straw hat. After borrowing some make-up from my mom, I was a scary clown. Perfect.

My friends were already waiting for me when I arrived. Harland was dressed like a mummy. He was covered head to toe with toilet paper. Bryce was dressed up like a creepy scarecrow and Jarrin was dressed like a zombie. We looked great.

"Let's hit the houses while the treats are flowing," Jarrin said.

"Dang. I forgot the toilet paper for the houses who give us bad treats," Bryce said.

"No need to worry. We can always use Harland's costume," I said.

"Ha-ha, very funny Shaun," he replied.

**We** spent about an hour trick or treating and had pretty full bags, but I guess it wasn't enough for Bryce.

"Let's steal some candy from little kids," he said.

"Dude, that's not cool," I answered.

"Come on. Everyone does it," Jarrin said.

"Little kids will be with their parents. It will never work," Harland said and I was grateful. I didn't want to steal from little kids.

"Then let's steal from big kids," Jarrin said as he approached three boys who were about our age.

Bryce and Jarrin cornered the boys up against a tree. "What are you guys supposed to be?" Jarrin laughed at them.

The biggest boy replied, "We are gypsies."

"Gypsies, how lame!" Bryce laughed.

"Now give us all your candy," Jarrin demanded.

The smallest boy held out his bag of goodies. It was a pillowcase that was worn and shabby.

"That's it?" Jarrin asked. "For all three of you? You are sharing one bag?"

The middle boy answered. "The smallest bite can bring pleasure to the tongue, but a greedy man who gobbles, tastes nothing."

"Whatever. Just hand it over," Jarrin said.

"Why don't you leave them alone, Jarrin? We have plenty," I said.

"Says who? Not me. What about you, Bryce? Do you have plenty?" Jarrin asked.

"Nope. I could use some more," Bryce added.

I looked at the three boys again. They looked alike; they could be brothers. They had olive skin, black hair, and dark eyes. Their clothes were tattered and torn, and their shoes had holes. Pretty convincing costumes, really.

The oldest boy grabbed the bag from the

youngest boy, removed one small candy bar, and tossed the bag to Jarrin. He unwrapped the candy bar and divided it into three pieces sharing it with the other two boys. A very kind thing to do and also a bit brave.

"Wise choice," Jarrin said. "You get to keep your teeth." Jarrin held up his fist to scare them, but it didn't rattle any of the boys.

I felt really bad about taking their candy. I knew Jarrin had a mean streak, but usually he kept it at harmless bullying. I'd noticed lately he was becoming meaner though.

"Give it back, Jarrin," Harland said.

"Why don't you make me?" he answered and pushed Harland.

Harland was the biggest guy out of all of us. I knew he could take Jarrin. He went to push him back and the oldest gypsy boy grabbed his arm.

"It's okay," he said. "We're leaving."

"I'm leaving, too," Harland said. "And I'm done hanging out with you two thugs," he added, looking right at Bryce and Jarrin.

"What about you, Shaun?" he asked.

"Yeah, Shaun. Are you going to hang with these losers or stay with us?" Jarrin jeered.

I knew the decision I made now would have big consequences. Jarrin was easily the most popular boy in school. Of course, most kids were scared of him, so that may have been why. I knew if I crossed him, I would no longer be part of the "A" crowd. Harland had been my friend since kindergarten. He was big and dorky, but he was a true friend.

"I'm with Harland," I said.

"Oh really? Then you can leave your candy with us too!" he said and pulled a switchblade out of his pocket.

Wow! That got out of hand quick. I threw my candy at him and ran. Harland was on my heels. The three gypsy boys just strolled away like they had all the time in the world.

After about a half a block, we stopped to catch our breath. The three gypsy boys came around the corner.

"You guys alright?" the oldest one asked.

"We're okay," I answered, gasping for breath.

"You made a very wise choice tonight," the middle one said.

"Not really," I answered, finally getting my breath back. "We made a bad enemy I fear."

The littlest boy just started laughing when

I said this. Soon, the other two were laughing too. They strolled away like they weren't afraid of anything. It was a little bit creepy.

Harland and I walked home with heavy hearts at losing our Halloween booty and becoming "B" listers. I couldn't help but worry what would happen Monday morning at school, now that we were on Jarrin's enemy list.

**On** Monday, I entered my homeroom class cautiously. I fully expected Jarrin to dog me about Halloween night. I was scared he'd try to knife me. I was relieved to find he and Bryce were both absent.

I sat next to Harland and sighed. Just then, Shikeria bounced over to us. She always had the best gossip.

"OMG! Did you hear what happened to Jarrin and Bryce?" she practically gasped.

"No," I answered.

"They were eating candy from an old tattered bag and it was spiked with razor blades! It cut their tongues off! Now they have to eat through a tube!"

"Will they die?" Harland asked.

"I don't know," she answered.

All I could think of was what that poor

gypsy boy said: "The smallest bite can bring pleasure to the tongue, but a greedy man who gobbles, tastes nothing."

It seemed to me that Jarrin and Bryce had tasted their last treat.

# SPHINX

**Going** to a haunted house was always fun and tonight was going to be out of control. We had heard about a secret haunted house that was only for the most popular kids in middle school. It was on the outskirts of town and since none of us could legally drive yet, we decided to ride the five miles on our bikes.

I rode my bike over to Cindee's house and waited in her driveway, like we planned. I texted her, and she appeared pushing her bike from around the side of her house. Before we could sneak away, her neighbor, Edgar, confronted us. We'd secretly nicknamed him, Egghead because he was so smart. Well, it wasn't all that secret.

"What's up, Edgar?" I asked. I didn't

want to be rude, but I didn't want to talk to him. He wasn't popular like Cindee and me.

"The sky, the crime rate, college tuition." He laughed at his own joke. "I mean, not much. How are things with you, Ellie?"

"Okay. We were just heading out," I answered.

"Oh, where to?" he asked.

"Nowhere you want to go, Egghead," Cindee said kinda mean.

"Hey, I'm a fun guy. Gimme the opportunity," he said serenely.

"What?" I asked. Sometimes I didn't understand him.

"Tell me where you are going," he said.

Cindee and I both looked at each other. I didn't want to tell him, and I didn't think she did either.

After an uncomfortable silence, Cindee finally spoke, "Well, there's a haunted house in a barn outside of town. We're riding our bikes to it."

"I'm in!" He was gone in a flash.

"Cindee, noooo! Why did you tell him? I don't want to be seen with him," I whined.

"I didn't think he would go for it. I thought he would be scared of haunted houses. He seems so wimpy," she said.

In no time at all, Egghead was riding his bike out of the garage. Since there was no way to back down now, we rode alongside him. He talked the whole time. At first it was annoying, but as the time went along, it kept me from thinking about how long and tiring the ride was. He was more interesting than I thought. Cindee rolled her eyes every time he started a new conversation. I guess she had probably heard it all before since she's lived next to him her whole life.

At last we arrived. We parked our bikes next to the other ones. It looked like the haunted house was a good half mile away up a steep hill. Maybe that's why everyone left their bikes here, because it was too hard to pedal up that hill. We started our trek and soon enough, I felt butterflies in my stomach. I wondered how scary this house was going to be. There weren't any streetlights out here in the country, but the moon was high and bright.

"I don't hear anything." Egghead said.

Very weird. I was thinking the exact same thing. *Why weren't there kids running all around, or scary music being played?* "I dunno," I said quietly.

"They all must be in the house," Cindee

said.

We all nodded our heads in agreement, although I don't think either one of us believed that explanation.

There was a single light bulb hanging by a thin wire that ran across the barn door. Next to the door was a bucket with a sign on it that read, "HAUNTED HOUSE TOURS $5!"

I only had a ten dollar bill on me. "Do either of you have a five dollar bill?" I asked.

"I do," Egghead said.

He handed me the five dollar bill and I placed the ten dollars in the bucket for both of us. We looked at Cindee.

"What? I'm not paying until I know it's worth it. Plus, how would anyone know? There isn't anyone here."

The butterflies in my stomach were now doing flip-flops.

Cindee pushed her way through the door, we followed closely behind. All that I could see was a sign with an arrow that said, *Go this way to answer the riddle.*

"What kinda haunted house is this?" Cindee said. "I'm so glad I didn't pay for it."

"I love riddles," Egghead announced.

I found myself standing closer to Egghead than Cindee. "Maybe we should follow that arrow." I pointed in the direction of the arrow.

Egghead grabbed my hand and tried to grab Cindee's, but she wouldn't take it. I did.

The arrow lead us to a small door. It was so small that we had to bend down to go through it. On the other side of the door was a cage. It looked like a sleeping animal was in it. Very good special effects, I thought. The body of the animal looked like a lion, but it had huge wings like a bird and the face looked like a cross between a woman and a cat. It was the strangest thing I had ever seen.

"What is that supposed to be?" Cindee asked aloud.

"I do believe it is a Sphinx," Egghead told us.

"A what?" I asked.

"A Sphinx. It was a mythological creature that guarded the entrance to the Greek city of Thebes. She would ask a riddle to travelers. If they answered correctly she allowed them passage through."

"And if they didn't answer right, what would happen?" I asked quietly. My hands were on my stomach in attempt to quiet the loud, gurgling noises.

"If they answered wrong, she would kill them. If they answered correctly, she would kill herself."

"Fascinating," Cindee said, "Too bad she isn't real. Although she looks it. Great costume!" Cindee proceeded to bang on the cage over and over.

In a flash, the Sphinx was awake and screeching at us! It was real! Or was it? Either way, we all backed away and Cindee headed back to the little door behind us.

"It's locked, we can't get out!" There was real fear in her voice.

"Of course, you can't get out! You each have a riddle to answer!" The Sphinx's voice was raspy. "You first, blondie." The Sphinx nodded in Cindee's direction.

"No thanks, I want get outta here!" she screamed.

"There is only one way out. Answer my riddle." The Sphinx spread her wings and let out a small yelp. "What is large as a mountain, small as a pea, but endlessly swims in a waterless sea?" She flapped her wings with excitement.

Cindee just stood there with her mouth open. I know she didn't know the answer. I didn't know the answer. I don't even know if Egghead knew the answer. Oh my gosh! She was going to kill Cindee! I looked to Egghead for help.

He stepped up close to the Sphinx. "I think I know the answer. May I answer it for Cindee?"

I could hear Cindee sigh with relief.

"Although that is a brave and honorable request, I must deny it," the Sphinx said. "I'm waiting for your answer."

Cindee looked at me and then at Egghead. She quietly mumbled, "Hope?"

The Sphinx said to Cindee, "That is incorrect; however, I do like your answer and it does answer the riddle. The correct answer is asteroids. Step aside until I can figure out what to do with you!"

Cindee sobbed quietly in the corner.

"You!" The Sphinx nodded at me. "I do not breathe, but I can jump. I do not eat, but I can stretch. I do not think, but I grow and play. I do not see, but you see me every day. What am I?"

I thought long and hard. It was very

tricky. It could be so many things. I didn't want to get this wrong.

Always the gentleman, Egghead stepped up to the Sphinx. "I know the answer, may I answer for Ellie?"

"I'm very surprised by your valor and bravery. No one has ever offered to answer for another and you have chosen to do it twice. You would have made an impressive knight, but still the answer is no."

I hugged Egghead. That was so nice of him. When I hugged him, he whispered in my ear.

"The answer is water!" I said. I winked at Edgar. It seemed wrong to keeping calling him Egghead at this point.

"Interesting, very interesting. That is not the correct answer. The answer is a leg! However, like your blubbering friend in the corner, I like your answer. It could also work. Go stand next to her and await further instructions. But someone will die tonight, mark my words."

"May I offer you a trade of sorts?" Edgar asked the Sphinx.

"I'm intrigued. Go on." She mewed and flapped her wings.

"If I answer your riddle correctly, you let

all of us go. If not, you kill me and let the girls go. This is really more in your favor than mine. Since you are still alive, I assume that no one has answered a riddle correctly tonight." Edgar said.

"No, Edgar!" I screamed.

"Let him! Either way we are out of here! Think of yourself," Cindee said.

The Sphinx rose higher on her lioness haunches. "It seems the fair maidens are in disaccord. One who thinks only of herself and the other seems to care for you. This is delightful. I will agree to it. But I must warn you; this next riddle has only one correct answer. Are you still confident in your offer?"

"I am!" Edgar exclaimed. Small beads of perspiration formed on his brow. He wiped them away.

"What has four legs in the morning, two legs in the afternoon, and three legs in the evening?"

This was a much harder riddle than either of us got. I knew that Edgar was thinking really hard. He was pacing back and forth in the room, mumbling to himself.

"I'm waiting," the Sphinx said.

Edgar stepped right up to the cage. He

was eye to eye with the hideous creature. I realized then and there that he wasn't like the other boys. None of the popular kids would have ever sacrificed their life for me. Never. And here he was, doing that exact thing for two girls who would barely give him the time of day. If we made it out alive, I decided that I would give him a chance and I would dump Cindee as my friend because she was so incredibly selfish.

"You are right, there is only one answer. Are you ready to die?" Edgar said confidently.

"Don't flatter yourself. Only one person in history has every answered that correctly, I have been told." The Sphinx smiled evilly. "The odds are not in your favor."

"I don't need odds when I have a brain. The answer is a man! He walks on all fours as a baby, he walks on two legs as an adult and when he gets old, he uses a cane."

Eerie silence filled the small room. The Sphinx's body started contorting, and she was having trouble breathing. It was as if the life was being squeezed out of her. "Well played my worthy adversary. You may all pass through." Those were her final words before she crumbled into a heap in the cage.

I threw my arms around Edgar's neck, and planted the biggest kiss ever, right on his mouth. He actually blushed!

The little door swung open and we all hurried through it as if our lives depended on it. I wasn't taking any more chances. I will never visit another haunted house again. As we were running down the hill, Cindee turned around and headed back to the barn.

"No, Cindee. Don't go back!" I yelled.

"We're free, Cindee. Come on!" Edgar yelled also.

She pulled out five dollars and placed it in the bucket and headed back down the hill. When she reached us, she said, "Just in case someone *was* watching."

# HERO

**Working** the night shift at a hospital emergency room as a nurse can go one of two ways. Super slow. I mean, so slow it feels like time stops. Or so busy, I don't have time to sit down.

It was Halloween night. What I wouldn't give to be eleven again going house to house ringing the bell and saying, "Trick or Treat!" Of course, I would usually be dressed up as a nurse. Sometimes even a scary nurse with fake blood all over my white scrubs and vampire teeth for an added spooky effect. Tonight, I had blood, but it was real. I was already on my second set of scrubs.

I sighed and glanced at my hot dinner. It would turn cold before I could take a break. My trauma pager went off with a loud beep again. This time alerting me that a gunshot wound will be arriving soon. And a car accident patient just rolled through the double doors, bringing in rain as well as sounds of the howling wind. Halloween; perfect weather for ghosts and ghouls.

I saw the paramedics roll a scruffy looking old man into Bay 13. Lucky number thirteen. Great.

The cute paramedic recited his injuries. His rain soaked jacket and hair dripped water over his pad as he wrote.

"Vital signs are good. He was found wandering around out in the rain. He seemed confused and didn't know who he was," he said, "There are no signs of being hit by a car or attacked by some Halloween pranksters, thank God."

I thanked the paramedic and wished him good luck out there. As he was leaving, he reached in his pocket and tossed me a candy bar. How did he know I was famished? I put the delicious treat in my white nurse's jacket for later.

I was alone with the mysterious man. I needed some information from him, so I could quickly treat him and get ready for the gunshot victim about to roll in.

"Hello, sir? Can you hear me? My name is Vivian Dahl and I'm a nurse here to help you. Do you know where you are?" I said in my calm voice, gently laying my hand upon his arm to reassure him I meant no harm.

He slowly turned to me with deep dark eyes. I felt like I should be scared, but his gaze was comforting like an old friend. Slowly, he began to speak, "Yes, I know where I am and I know who I am." With that, he pulled the blankets up to his neck like he hadn't been warm in years.

I felt a cold chill rush through the room and quickly thought, *Why is it so cold in here?* I chalked it up to the automatic air conditioner coming on again. They always keep it so cold in here, it's a wonder anyone can get warm.

"So, are you going to share your name with me because I don't have time to guess what it is. The sooner you help me out, the sooner I can help you," I said a little impatiently.

This time the old man sat up slowly and whispered, "You like taking care of people? Helping them out? Putting their needs first over yours?"

With that he laid back, like the act of just

sitting up wore him out.

I thought that maybe he just wanted a friend to talk to, or just wanted out of the rain for a while. I had to stop and take a breath. I glanced down into my pocket looking at that candy bar waiting to be eaten.

"Go ahead, eat your treat," he said.

*How did he know what was in my pocket?*

"No sir, I won't eat until I can find out why you're here. I take my job seriously and I really need to know if you're ok."

With that, my stomach growled and I swore I heard a faint chuckle from under his breath. Who knows the last time he had at bath, or a decent meal for that matter? Either way, I always treated everyone the same, with respect and dignity. No matter what.

I checked his vital signs again and they all looked normal. He was really cold to the touch. Unusually cold. It made me nervous.

"I need to order some tests and take some blood," I said.

"No!" he shouted, "No blood! No tests! I won't be here for that long."

Something about his insistence made my skin crawl. Either he was afraid of getting his blood drawn, or he knew something I didn't.

My face must have shown signs of panic because he then spoke calmly to me.

"I'll explain, if you promise not to get a doctor and start poking me with needles."

I agreed for the time being, giving him the benefit of the doubt. I figured he had a fear of needles. He wouldn't have been the first. The last thing I wanted to do was physically restrain him to the bed to force tests that could be unnecessary. I thought taking the easy route would work out better, and then I could move on to the gunshot victim who had already been rolled into Trauma Bay 3. It was much warmer in there. It's always set extra warm for true traumas so the patients don't go into shock. I actually welcomed the hustle and bustle of the warm room instead of this freezing one. I pulled my nurse's jacket tighter.

"Ok, I'm waiting," I said, trying hard not to roll my eyes. I figured I was about to hear a load of malarkey.

The old man raised his scrawny arm and gestured for me to lean closely to his ear. Normally, I wouldn't get so close, but something told me to agree to this. As I leaned in closer, I swear I felt even colder.

He whispered, "I know you, Vivian Dahl," he said slowly, but with determination. "I've known you for many years".

A chill went up my spine and the hairs on the back of my neck stood up straight. Impossible! I would remember such a fellow and I didn't have any long lost uncles or cousins either. *How would he know me?*

I knew now, without a doubt that he was a loon. The old man had lost his mind. And I was stuck with him until he could be sent to the psychiatric unit. My dinner was really going to be cold.

Now I did roll my eyes. I was about to turn and get some help when he shouted, "Do you remember Halloween night, ten years ago?"

I stopped in my tracks and quickly turned around, dropping his chart and my pen. "What?" was all I could manage to say.

"I know you remember what happened that night," he said, not harshly, but with compassion and sadness in his voice.

I quickly thought back to that horrid night when my mom, dad and I were coming home from a Halloween party at my aunt's house. The night was stormy, just like tonight. I had had such a fun time at my aunt's party with all my cousins. I was grateful that we had games and food inside, because it was just too wet to trick or treat.

That was the last Halloween I celebrated. Not only because I was twelve and too old to Trick or Treat, but that was the night I lost my parents and was almost killed myself. We were driving home around 11:00 p.m., and the roads were slick with rain. Suddenly, a deer leapt out in front of our car. It all happened so fast, I thought it was a dream until I woke up in the children's hospital. I had a broken leg and some burns, but nothing so bad a few weeks in the hospital wouldn't cure.

I remember how sad I was that I had lost my parents in the car crash. The nurses and doctors were so good to me, that I promised then and there to help give back one day. I had always wanted to be a nurse, but that sealed the deal.

I still don't remember how I got out of the car with a broken leg and flames leaping up around me. I could smell the smoke and tried to scream, but I don't think any sound came out.

I found out later that the paramedics had put in their report that when they came upon the accident, I was laying on the grass safely wrapped in a blanket. I don't recall how I did that or how I escaped from the burning wreck, but I did. I only wish my parents could have done the same. My aunt raised me and I went on to have the best childhood I could with loving relatives and a good education. I never looked back or felt sorry for myself. I couldn't; this job kept you in check. Just when you started to feel bad, someone always had it worse. I snapped back to reality and looked at this poor home-less man with a puzzled look on my face.

"How did you know what happened to me that night?" I asked with anticipation.

His dark eyes looked deep in mine and said, "I was the one who pulled you to safety and wrapped you in a blanket. Your mom and dad were already dead when I pried open the car door. I heard you screaming and I wanted to save you. Even though it meant I would most likely die myself. When I saw you in that nurse's costume, well, I just knew you would grow up to help others. I couldn't let a selfless soul like you die."

*How did he know what costume I was wearing?*

I shook my head to try to clear it. Was I

hearing this right? No one saved me that night. I hobbled out myself. I was wrapped up in a blanket, but figured maybe a cop put one on me. No! They said they found me wrapped in a blanket when they arrived. Why hadn't I heard about this hero before?

"If this is true, why haven't I heard about you and why are you here now, telling me this?"

He sat up and said, "I wanted to see if you grew up to be a good person. I had to know if it was worth it."

*If it was worth it? Why wouldn't it have been worth saving someone from certain death?*

"I can't thank you enough," was all I could say over and over.

He just looked at me encouraging me to go on, so I told him about my aunt raising me and how I dedicated my life to helping others. His blanket slipped to the floor.

"Let me get you a fresh warm blanket. That's the least I can do for my hero." I said.

Before I left, I gave him my candy bar from my pocket and he reached out, but instead of taking the candy right away, he held my hand. I felt the warmth finally come back to his icy skin. I paused and smiled and reassured him that I'd be right back.

I came back and opened the curtain to his room with the warm blanket still under my arm, but there was no one there! He left? How will I ever know his name? Will he be ok?

I thought about what he'd said earlier, "I won't be around for that long." Did he mean he was dying or just wanted to see me and this was the only way? I sat down in the warm room. Finally, the AC must have shut off. I smelled a faint scent of smoke, like from a fire. Weird. Well, at least he took the candy with him; he looked like he could use a bite to eat.

I had to get back to another patient. I continued my busy evening, but my mind wandered back to the old man. How did he know my name? Or where I worked? It made me feel uneasy.

Later that evening, I ran into a childhood friend, Chris. He worked at the hospital too, but as a paramedic. I ran up to him and blurted out, "Your dad was the cop on the scene of my accident, right?" Even though I already knew the answer. It always made Chris uncomfortable talking about it, but this time I needed answers.

"Yes, of course…you know that," he said reluctantly.

"I just had the strangest encounter tonight," I whispered. "I met an old scruffy man who claims he pulled me out of the burning car and wrapped me in a blanket."

Chris's eyes widened. "No, can't be. Are you sure?"

"Yes. I'm telling you, this man knew details about me that he could not have known." I was almost in tears now. I had to know the truth.

Chris took both of my hands in his and started to explain.

"My dad once told me a few years ago, about that night. I didn't want to tell you and upset you even more."

"What could possibly upset me more than losing my parents?" I was holding my breath waiting for Chris's response.

He looked directly at me and said, "A homeless man dragged you out of the burning car and wrapped his blanket around you to keep you dry from the rain. When my father arrived in his police car, he found you safe away from the burning car."

I gasped, that was the old man tonight! He did save me. I knew I felt a familiar connection to this strange man.

Chris grabbed my hands tighter and spoke low and slowly, "That homeless man died right next to you from smoke inhalation and burns. He was buried in an unmarked grave outside of town. The person you say you saw tonight must have been his ghost!"

The tears came running down my face and I must have been ready to faint because the next thing I knew, I woke up in one of our ER beds and it was morning. I pulled myself together and left to go home.

Something made me turn down the street of the old graveyard. The sun was just coming up and the rain had made everything clean and fresh. I don't know why I wanted to walk around the graveyard; it seemed like a dream last night. I turned to walk back to my car when a reflection of something caught my eye. I walked over to a simple gravesite. It was a plain tombstone with no name, only a date which read, *Died, October 31$^{st}$, 2002.*

I looked down and saw, placed by the stone, an uneaten candy bar just like the one I offered my hero last night.

# TRUTH

**It** was the night before Halloween and I was sitting around a bonfire with two of my best friends and my cousin Aimee who was visiting for a few days. The air was cool and every once in a while a strong wind would whip up. My mom had given us all the ingredients to make S'mores. We hadn't started yet because Aimee was telling us about a game called Truth, Dare or Double-dare.

"I'm in," Cissy said.

"Me too," chimed Vanessa.

They were staring at me. "Well, Kenzie?" Aimee asked me.

It sounded fun, but I was a little leery. "What happens again if you get caught lying if you pick truth?"

"Oh, that's the worst! They say if you're lying, then by morning something horrible will happen to you," Aimee explained.

I've never been much of a liar, but I'm not perfect. I guess I would be safe. I knew that sometimes Cissy would lie and that Vanessa didn't lie, but would sometimes exaggerate the truth. "Okay, let's do it!" I said.

"I'll ask first." Aimee took charge. "Okay, Vanessa, truth, dare or doubledare?"

Vanessa pondered a moment and said, "Dare."

Aimee laughed. "Sweet! You have to make three S'mores and eat them all in under one minute. I will time you."

Vanessa's eyes grew wide. "I don't know if I can."

"You have to try, it's a dare," Cissy said.

We helped Vanessa make the S'mores, plus we wanted some too. After we assembled a number of them, Aimee started the count down. Vanessa greedily ate the first one and gave us the thumbs up sign. The second one didn't go down as fast, but she still had plenty of time. She was having trouble with the third one, but with two seconds left, she swallowed the last remaining bite. She did it!

"Good job, Vanes…" Before I could finish, Vanessa was bent over the bonfire spewing chunks of graham crackers, marshmallows and chocolate.

"EEEEWWW!" we all said in unison.

Vanessa wiped her mouth with the back of her jacket sleeve. She took a swig of water, swished it around her mouth and spit it out. "My turn. Cissy, truth, dare or doubledare?"

Cissy said, "Truth, truth."

I couldn't blame Cissy after watching Vanessa's dare.

"How old were you when you kissed a boy for the first time?" Vanessa asked.

I knew the answer to that. It was just last week with Jason. She'd had a crush on him for forever. Back in the fifth grade, she made me pinkie swear that I would never kiss him no matter what because she was so in love with him.

Cissy sighed with relief at the easy question. "That would be last week with Jason, and I'm almost thirteen…in two more weeks." She said that for the benefit of Aimee, as we already knew her birthday.

"Aimee, truth, dare or doubledare?" Cissy

asked.

"Doubledare!" Aimee said without hesitation.

Cissy turned her head toward the side of the house. Even in the dark, I could tell what she was looking at. My mom's prized Autumn Joy plants. My mom had explained to us earlier how much she loved them and even though they had pink flowers on them now, they would turn to a coppery color and then red in time for winter.

"Aimee, you have to destroy at least one of Kenzie's mom's Autumn Joy plants."

"No!" I screamed. This game was getting out of control. "Do you know how much trouble I will be in?"

"Cissy's right. It has to be bad, it's a doubledare." Vanessa explained.

"I'll do it!" Aimee said and marched over to the plants. We hastily followed.

Aimee proceeded to stomp on the biggest bush. My stomach started to hurt just looking at it. My mom would be heartbroken. Everyone else just laughed. We headed back toward the bonfire.

"Your turn, Kenzie," Aimee smirked.

I was too scared to say dare, because I didn't know if any more dares would end up destroying more of our house. "Truth," I said but all the fun of the game was gone for me.

"Who was the last boy you kissed?" Aimee asked me.

Oh no, this can't be happening. I should have said dare and suffered the consequences with my mother. My girlfriends knew I was kind of a tease when it came to kissing. What can I say, it's fun. I have probably kissed more boys than any other girl in middle school. I have even kissed a boy in high school. I didn't want to tell them the truth because it would have broken Cissy's heart and destroyed our friendship. Yes, I kissed Jason. I couldn't help it. I didn't plan for it to happen, it just did. The truth was, he wasn't that great of a kisser. I regretted it instantly. There was no way I was telling the truth.

"Oh, that's an easy one. It was Freddy. He's been flirting with me for a while now. I thought, what the heck." It was true that Freddy had been flirting with me, but I had no desire to kiss him.

"So, Freddy, huh?" Aimee asked.

"Yeah, Freddy." What was up with that? No one else got hassled after their turn. Why was I? I just wanted this game to end.

As if on cue, a cold wind whipped by and the skies opened up. It started raining and I swear it dropped at least twenty degrees.

"Ugh, let's get inside." Cissy cried.

We didn't even have to put the bonfire out. The rain took care of that. The crack of lightening and the boom of thunder sent us all running into the house. I quickly glanced at the Autumn Joy bush that was mangled. Maybe Mom would think the storm did it.

As we dried ourselves off in my room, the girls couldn't stop talking about Cissy kissing Jason. Really? I kept trying to steer the conversation to clothes or music, but they kept ignoring me.

"I really, really like him." Cissy kept repeating over and over.

"Yeah, he sounds great. Maybe you can be his girlfriend." Aimee offered.

"I don't think he is seeing anyone right now," Vanessa said. "Although when I heard he made out with someone in the media center, I didn't know it was you! How exciting!"

"What? I did not kiss him in the media center. It was outside near the buses. Who did he kiss in the media center?" Cissy said practically yelling.

The pit in my stomach grew bigger. Who saw us kissing in the media center? I swear there were eyes everywhere at that school.

"I'm sure it was nothing. I bet he really liked kissing you more. Who cares who the other girl was?" I said.

This seemed to calm her down a bit. I didn't know what to do. Should I confess or keep my mouth shut? I had no feelings for Jason and I knew how much Cissy liked him. Also, I was a bit worried about something bad happening to me because I didn't tell the truth. No wait; that was just the stupid game.

My mom brought us some hot chocolate.

"Ouch!" I screamed. I burned my tongue on my first sip.

"Be careful, it's really hot," Vanessa said.

"Tanks for the warring," I slurred as my tongue started to swell. This can't happen. The big Halloween party was tomorrow night and I planned on doing a lot of kissing. All I wanted to do was go to sleep and forget this night.

When I woke up the next morning, my tongue was back to its normal size. Thank goodness. I had been thinking about Freddy.

Maybe I did want to kiss him after all.

The breakfast table was abuzz with lots of chatter. My mom had gone all out and decorated the house while we slept. There were spider webs hanging in the corners and bowls of candy corn on the table. She even made us pancakes that looked like Jack-O-Lanterns. She was in a good mood; I guess she hadn't seen her trampled bush yet. The sky was overcast, which was perfect for Halloween day. She had left us dozens of Halloween cookies for us to decorate later. That would be fun.

"I'm going out for a bit. Will you girls be okay by yourselves?" my mom asked us.

How embarrassing! "Of course, we will be okay. What could happen?" I asked.

"I know. It's just that it's Halloween and you never know," she said laughing. She grabbed her purse and headed out.

"Pass the syrup," Vanessa said to Aimee who was drowning her pancakes in it.

Aimee threw it to Vanessa, who didn't catch it, and it dropped on the floor. Syrup slowly spread out all over the tile. I quickly sopped it up with some paper towels.

"Come on guys, be careful," I said.

"Yeah, stop throwing things. Somebody

could get hurt...or sticky," Cissy said and laughed. She threw a candy corn at Aimee. Aimee caught it in her mouth.

"You know I can juggle, right?" Cissy said.

"Prove it." Aimee challenged.

Cissy grabbed three oranges and started juggling. Hey, she was pretty good!

"My uncle taught me when I was little. It's not hard," Cissy said.

"Can you juggle bigger, scarier objects?" Vanessa asked.

I did not like where this was heading. "What's wrong with the oranges?" I asked.

"Yeah, I bet I could juggle those knives over there." Cissy was looking at the knives in my mom's knife block.

"No!" I screamed.

"Yeaah!" Vanessa and Aimee yelled.

Cissy grabbed three knifes: one really big one and two smaller ones. To her credit, she was juggling really well. The knives flew in the air and she caught them by their handles and effortlessly tossed them back up. Very impressive. We all cheered her on. Just then, the phone rang and she lost her concentration. The big knife plunged downward straight for my hand that was resting on the table. I didn't have time to react. It slit my pinkie finger clean off! My little finger went flying into the air in slow motion.

What happened next was a blur. I was hyperventilating and could hear the sound of sirens. Aimee was packing something in ice in a ziplock bag. *Was it my finger?* I don't know because I passed out.

I woke up in the ambulance and Cissy was in there with me. I wasn't in any pain. They must have given me something. My brain was a little fuzzy. I kept repeating, "Pinkie swear, pinkie swear…"

"What are you talking about?" Cissy asked me.

"Pinkie swear with you!" I mumbled.

"Your pinkie is in a cooler. They said it can be reattached. I'm so sorry. How can I make it up to you?" Cissy broke down crying.

"No, I lied. That's why I lost my pinkie. I lied in the game last night."

"What are you talking about now? You are delirious." Cissy tried to comfort me.

I had to tell her now or I never would. It was risky; I could lose her friendship forever.

"It was me in the media center."

"What? I think you're delirious!" she said.

"I kissed Jason in the media center." I admitted it and it felt great, like a big weight was lifted off my chest. I slowly slipped into unconsciousness with my conscience finally clean.

**Later** that day, as I sat in the hospital bed eating strawberry Jell-O, Cissy bounced into my room.

"How's the finger?" she asked.

"The doctor reattached it, but said it will have limited use."

"So no more pinkie swears?" she asked.

"No. I guess not. I'm really sorry about Jason."

"You know, I already knew."

"You did?"

"Yeah. He actually told me himself. He said he wanted to be my boyfriend and didn't want any lies between us."

"Oh. Why didn't you say you knew?"

"I wanted to see if you would admit it to me. I guess I was testing your honesty. And you passed."

I wanted to tell Cissy I only told her because I was afraid I'd lose my pinkie completely. But I really did feel better after I came clean.

"So you're not mad?" I asked.

"I was a little until..." she trailed off.

"Until what?" I asked.

"Well, it's kinda all over school. He said you were a really bad kisser."

What? I was about to tell her that he was the one who was a bad kisser, but I figured I'd done enough damage already. One thing was for sure, I'd never play Truth, Dare or Doubledare again. And that's the truth!

# BOXCAR

*Some mysteries take several years before their secrets are revealed. This is one of those stories.*

**I** was thirteen years old in the summer of 1977. One afternoon, my mother had just about enough of three daughters underfoot all day. She sent us on an errand to the neighborhood grocery store. We spilled out of the house, grateful for some freedom on a sunny day.

Rose, being fourteen and thus the oldest, was officially in charge of me and my little sister, Ann, who was ten. My father called Ann his "Little Tiger" because she was fearless. If she smelled an adventure, no one could stop her. Especially Rose, as she found out later that day.

Now, normally you would exit our house, walk down the driveway and turn right onto the sidewalk to go to the store. You would follow the sidewalk for one block, where you would promptly turned right again and walked another block. The sidewalk ended in the parking lot of the local grocery store, but that was not the way we went.

Without so much as breathing a word to each other, we all turned left at the end of the drive. From there, it was just a quick right at the end of the block and then a straight shot to the back of the grocery store via an old dirt road.

The old dirt road was quicker, but somehow it wasn't. It probably had to do with the fact that we stopped frequently to examine a shiny rock or a piece of bone. Many a time, we were convinced we'd found a real treasure. A few years back, when Rose was twelve, she was positive she'd found a dinosaur bone. Rose even took it to her sixth grade teacher, Mr. Madron, to see if it were real. He just chuckled and said it was a beef bone. But he told Rose she could bring any treasure in she found and he would help her identify it. He was good to his word, too.

When I was in his class the next year, I brought him what I thought was a rough diamond. He identified it as a white quartz crystal and told me to keep treasure hunting with my sisters.

As we walked that day, we felt free like kids do when there are no grownups around. We picked up small rocks, examined them and chucked them aside. Off in the distance, we heard a train whistle blow. We stopped short of the train tracks, which crossed the old dirt road. It had long been a game of ours to count the cars as they passed.

As the train approached with all its clacks, clanks, and whistles, we stood by and started counting. At thirty cars, the train began to slow. And then suddenly, it stopped. An open boxcar faced us and we tried to peer into its shadowy depths. Ann couldn't resist the temptation and jumped on board.

"Get out of there, now!" Rose screamed at her with no avail.

Ann popped her head out and smiled and then ducked back in.

"I'm telling Mom!" Rose threatened, but I knew she was bluffing. Rose wouldn't tell Mom because then it would look like she couldn't control my sister; which really she couldn't.

Finally, Rose had had enough, and in two quick steps, her long legs hoisted her up to the boxcar with Ann. Not to be left out, I scrambled in too, though it took my chubby legs more than two steps. Once inside, it smelled sour and dank.

"Get out of here now!" Rose demanded as Ann danced in and out of her grip.

"Sisters shouldn't fight," an old gravelly voice said from the shadowed corner of the boxcar.

We all jumped out of our skins as an old hobo peered from the darkness. His eyes could only be described as ice blue. They pierced right into your very soul.

He pointed his old, gnarled and dirty finger at Rose and whispered two words, "Silver Wings".

Rose gave me a side-long glance that implied, *let's get out of here.*

Then, his icy eyes turned on me, and I was convinced he could read my mind. He whispered, "Painted Apple."

At this point, Ann had reached into her pocket for the loose change she was saving for a candy bar. She cautiously approached the old bum with her hand out.

"Ann, let's go." I heard the strain in Rose's voice. Her body language was flexed to move, and I knew she could be between Ann and the old man in a stride and a half. Forever, the big sister protector.

"Take this," Ann said, as she held the money out for the old man.

He snatched it quick and grabbed Ann's hand in the process. "Bloody Scalpel!" he screamed at Ann. She twisted free from his grip and leapt out of the boxcar. Rose and I were quick to follow. As if on cue, the train began lumbering along again.

We all stood in a daze for a moment, half scared out of our wits. We made a pact then and there, as only siblings can do, to never tell Mom what happened. We knew too many privileges would be taken away. We were smart enough to know a close call when we saw it and to learn from it.

We were very quiet and well behaved girls for the rest of the day, as you can imagine. If Mom knew something had happened to shake us up, she never said so. We pushed the scary memory to the back of our minds and didn't think about it for several years; until Halloween of this year.

We were adults by then and moms ourselves. My older sister, Rose, had just got off work as a flight attendant, and had just arrived at Ann's house for her Halloween bash. The house was full of screaming kids dressed up like monsters, princesses, and animals. They were running around and scaring each other at every turn. Squeals bounced off the walls and so did laughter. The noise didn't bother me much as I was an elementary art teacher and was used to noisy children.

Later that evening, after the last child had gone home or been put to bed, we sat around the dining table drinking coffee and reminiscing. Ann looked tired and said she had a hard day at work. She was a nurse in the ER. She rubbed her feet and sighed as I refilled her coffee.

"Remember Halloween when we were kids?" Rose asked.

"I sure do," I answered. "That was back when you could trick or treat without your parents along. It was a freer time to be a kid."

"I remember how exciting it was being out after dark and running around the neighborhood," Ann said.

"Me too," I said. "But it was never really

scary."

"No, not really. Not as scary as that time on that old boxcar." Ann added.

"I haven't thought of that in years!" Rose said. "I was so mad at you for jumping on that boxcar. You didn't listen to a thing I said."

"I know. I was a terror. But remember how scary that old bum was? He had eyes that pierced right through you."

"Yeah, and he said such bizarre things, remember?" Rose said.

Just then my face went completely white and I got goose bumps.

"What's wrong?" Ann asked, picking up on my change in pallor as only a nurse can.

"Do you guys remember what he said?" I asked.

"He said something about wings to me," Rose answered.

"He said 'Silver Wings,'" I said.

"Yes, that's right."

"And to me he said, 'Painted Apple,'" I recalled.

"He screamed at me, 'Bloody Scalpel,'" Ann said. "It was one of the few times I was really scared as a kid."

"Well get ready to be really creeped out,

because the old bum was telling our future," I announced.

"What?" they both said at once.

"'Silver Wings' he said to Rose and you're a flight attendant. You spend half your life in a silver plane. 'Painted Apple', he said to me and I'm an art teacher. An apple for the teacher, but painted, get it?"

They both nodded their heads.

"And 'Bloody Scalpel?' You just finished a shift in the ER. How's that for a bloody scalpel?"

Now my sisters turned pale as we sipped our coffee in silence and shuddered. From far away, we heard a train whistle blow.

# KARMA

**It** was a cool Saturday afternoon in October. I was walking around our local flea market with a couple of friends, hoping to find a buried treasure amidst all the junk. Somewhere close by I could smell burning leaves. The smoke mixed with the caramel corn vender creating an aroma that could only be described as fall.

"Hey Indi, check this out," my best friend, Brittnee, said as she dragged me over to a vendor with costume jewelry and colorful scarves on display.

The sign on her booth said, *Useful Items*. I wasn't sure how useful costume jewelry and scarves were, but I decided to check it out. An old Indian lady dressed in a bold sari sat behind the booth. She had beautiful dark eyes set into a craggy and wizened brown face. An emerald nose ring adorned her left nostril. She crooked her finger and gestured for me to come closer.

As I neared, colorful gemstones danced in the sunlight. I was mesmerized. I have to admit that I'm kind of a fashionista. I have the ability to take old clothes and jewelry and arrange them into a slammin' outfit. I've started a few trends at my school, I can tell you.

Brittnee picked up a gaudy pair of green and gold dangly earrings.

"What do you think?" she asked. She held them up to her ear lobes.

"Terrible for your ears. They're too old school, but they would make a great bauble for your cell phone."

"You're right! And green and gold are our school colors!" She squealed with delight as she forked over a couple of bucks for her new accessory.

"Always the cheerleader," I teased her.

I pawed through a cardboard box of necklaces like a pirate looking for buried treasure. After a minute, I struck gold, well silver anyway. I pulled out an old silver locket. It had a small sprig of indigo flowers engraved on it. I was meant to have it! Indigo wasn't only my name, but the color of my eyes. Not to be conceded, but I was really pretty. From my purple/blue eyes to my long black hair, I was easily the prettiest girl in school.

"How much for the locket?" I asked.

"It's not for sale," the old lady said.

"It was in the box marked *clearance*."

"That was a mistake," she answered.

I was only thirteen, but I was a savvy girl. I knew she was playing a game to get the best price for the locket. I decided to play along.

"Fair enough," I said, and tossed it back in the box. I began pawing through another box of ugly earrings.

"Perhaps I could let it go, if the price was right. Say, thirty dollars?"

The game was on, and I was a born haggler.

"Seems a bit pricey for a used locket." I sniffed and pretended to be interested in a gaudy pair of fuchsia earrings.

"I could take twenty, but I must warn you, the locket is not what it seems."

"No way! Is it magic?" Brittnee asked.

I could have told Brittnee it wasn't. It was

just a ploy to get me interested. Classic move. The old lady had good game. Supernatural jewelry? I don't think so.

"Magic? Sort of. It mirrors your karma. Whatever the wearer projects, will come back to them."

"Well, I would hate to buy a jinxed piece of jewelry. That kinda sounds like a rip off to me. Although, it is sort of pretty. I'll give you five dollars for it."

"Fifteen and it's yours," she countered.

From there the bidding war continued.

"Ten," I offered.

"Tell you what, little girl. I will give it to you for thirteen dollars, but you must promise to never return it to me

"Ah, okay," I said. What a weird old lady.

I handed her thirteen dollars, the last of my babysitting money, and grabbed the locket greedily.

As we were walking away from the booth, I heard her yell, "Remember, no returns!" She cackled like she just told the funniest joke in the world.

**Later** that night, Brittnee and I were in my room getting ready for a boy/girl party. Nyla Thompson was throwing the party. She was the second most popular girl in the school, after me, of course.

I brushed my gorgeous black hair. I fastened the silver locket around my neck. It hung beautifully over my indigo sweater, which of course matched my eyes. I had tried to open it earlier, to see what was inside, but it would not give up its secrets.

"You look great," Brittnee said.

"Duh," I said. Of course I looked great.

"How do I look?" she asked.

Brittnee was wearing a pumpkin color sweater. It had a pretty cut and probably cost a lot, but the pumpkin color was gross.

"You look okay," I said trying to be honest. I mean, her face and hair looked good, but that sweater? Hideous.

Brittnee looked hurt. Whatever. Then I noticed her lips turn up slightly into a smirk.

"Well, you do look good. I mean, aside from that huge pimple on your face," she said.

I spun around and glared at the mirror. Ugh! She was right. I had a big whitehead on the end of my nose! Where did that come from? It wasn't there a few minutes ago.

"You should probably pop that. It's hideous." She said, using the exact word I had thought of just a moment ago to describe her sweater.

I popped the pimple quickly, but my nose still had a swollen red bump. I tried applying concealer to cover it up. It helped, but not much.

**The** party was in full swing when we arrived. I made my rounds, saying hi to all the popular people. Nyla threw a good party, except she always invited everyone, even the unpopular kids. She even invited some sixth graders. Ew.

I went over to the punch bowl to help myself to a cup. A plump, sixth grade girl smiled at me.

"Isn't this a great party?" she asked.

"Mm hmm," I mumbled trying to give her a hint that I only conversed with popular people.

"I'm Greta. I'm in the sixth grade," she said.

I didn't answer.

"You're Indigo. Everybody knows you, you're so popular," she gushed.

"Thanks," I said. I could tell she was a *wannabe*. Ugh! I didn't want to encourage her.

"You should try the cupcakes. Nyla made them herself. I've already had two," she said as she handed me a gooey chocolate cupcake.

"Yuck! Too many calories," I said as I pushed it away. I didn't want to get fat like Greta. Even her hands were plump.

"Oh," she said and walked away defeated as if she could read my mind.

"Party favors!" Nyla announced. "Everyone grab a bag. If you don't like what you get, you can trade with a friend!"

Party favors was an old take on a kid's party idea that Nyla had revamped. Every time she threw a party, she hit the dollar store for kitschy party favors. They were cheap and gaudy, but everyone loved them because they were always in green and gold, our school colors. School spirit ran deep with this crowd.

Nyla circled around the room with little gold bags. Everyone had a blast opening them. The party buzzed for half an hour as the trading ensued.

I looked in my bag and knew I had to trade. It was chock full of green peanut M & M's. Empty calories. Plus, I had a peanut allergy. I figured I could trade with Greta;

she'd probably gobble them up.

"Yoohoo! Greta!" I called from across the room.

She ran over like a trained lapdog.

"Hi again!" she squealed. "What did you get?"

"A truly delicious treat. How 'bout you?" I asked.

"A mood ring. It's shaped like a hornet. Our school mascot. See, the mood stone is the hornet's body." She thrust her pinky finger under my nose and wiggled it for effect. "I think I'll keep it".

I had to have that. Too cool.

"Not bad," I said. "Although mood rings are traditionally worn on the ring finger."

Her face fell. She knew her ring finger was too pudgy for the ring to fit.

"Well, if that's true then we should trade. Is it true? Really? I know you would know because you are the best dressed girl in school."

"It really is true. Cross my heart," I said as I lied through my teeth.

She reluctantly took the ring off her finger and gave it to me. I slipped it on my finger and admired it.

"It looks good on me," I triumphantly said

and handed her my bag of peanut M & M's. As I was doing so, Jayden Shield, the class klutz bumped into me. Green peanut M & M's spilled out of the bag and rained onto my bejeweled hand.

"Watch where you're going! You're such a klutz!" I scolded.

Just then, the latest popular song came on and everyone yelled in delight and started to dance. I joined in the fun.

After dancing for several songs, I noticed my hand began to itch. When I looked down at it I screamed. Everyone stopped and stared. My hand was swelling up like a balloon.

"Oh my gosh! Your hand is so plump!" Greta said, using the exact word I had thought about her own hand.

"It is! It must have been the peanut M&M's! I'm allergic to peanuts!" I wailed. The ring was pinching my finger like crazy.

"We gotta get the swelling down before the ring pinches your finger off!" Brittnee said.

Nyla called for her mom who was a nurse. She tried to remove the ring by rubbing dish soap on it. It didn't budge. She immediately gave me an antihistamine pill. She made an ice pack and wrapped it in a cloth and placed it on my hand.

"I don't want to scare you, but if the swelling doesn't go down soon, you'll need to get to the doctor. I'm afraid that ring could cut off your circulation. I'm calling your mom," Nyla's mom said.

I sat down and tried not to panic. The party went on like everything was normal. Like I wasn't sitting there, possibly getting ready to lose a finger. I watched through the window for my mom. Finally, I saw her pull up. I ran to the door, bumping into the table on the way. I knocked over the punch bowl and shattered it into a million pieces. Food went flying everywhere.

"What a klutz!" Jayden said loudly and everyone laughed at me.

"I'm just drowsy from the antihistamine." I said, but no one heard over the laughter.

I stumbled out the door and into my car. I burst into tears.

My mom grabbed my hand and studied it. She pulled some lip gloss out of her bag and wiped it around the ring. She twisted it firmly and it came off.

"Alright. It's okay now. Obviously, the swelling has gone down a little or the ring wouldn't have come off," she said, but I couldn't stop crying.

I had been humiliated at the party. First the pimple. Then the swollen hand. Not to mention destroying the punchbowl and all the treats. I wiped my eyes and stared out the car window on the way home.

I kept replaying the night's events over and over. It was as if I were jinxed. Then I realized it was the locket! The old lady said it was a karma locket. Didn't she? I decided I would get to the bottom of the odd happenings. I would talk to the old lady next Saturday and make her tell me what to do.

The next week at school was the weirdest I'd ever experienced. I decided I would only think and say kind things, just in case the locket made more bad things happen. I didn't wear the locket, but I also didn't know how far its power extended. In fact, I didn't wear any jewelry at all. Just in case the locket's energy rubbed off on my other jewelry inside my jewelry box. I could not believe how quickly I had changed my tune about supernatural happenings.

I tried as hard as I could to not say or think bad thoughts of others. Still, by the end of the week, I had three more pimples and a weird fungus under my thumbnail. I knew the pimples were a consequence from every time I ran into Candace Smoot. She had really bad acne! I couldn't help but shudder when I saw her pizza face. And I had seen her three times this week.

I'm pretty sure I caught the nail fungus from Wayne Dorrin. I caught myself staring at his cruddy thumbnail in math class when I was supposed to be learning pre-algebra. Although I didn't touch him, I somehow got his fungus.

**Finally**, it was Saturday. Thank Goodness! I didn't think my skin could take much more. I called Brittnee up to see if she wanted to go to the flea market with me but she said she was hanging out with Nyla instead. I felt a little betrayed because that was our thing. Was Nyla her new best friend now?

I ran through the flea market to the old lady's booth, but she wasn't there. Instead, there was a very beautiful, middle-aged Indian woman.

"Excuse me. I'm looking for the old lady who was here last week. Maybe she was your mom?" I said. They did look alike.

"I thought you might be back," the lady

said.

I didn't quite understand what she was talking about, so I tried again. "Do you know where I can find the old lady who was here last Saturday?"

"I do."

"Will you tell me?" I asked.

"I do not think you are ready to hear," she answered.

"I don't mean to be rude, but things haven't been going too well for me lately and I need to speak with her. It's about this locket," I said and thrust the locket under her face.

"No returns! You could buy something else though," she cackled.

Something about that cackle reminded me of the old lady. Finally, my last nerve snapped. "I don't want to buy something else! This is all cheap junk! I'd rather wear rags! Now tell me where the old lady is!"

"Temper, temper. You must control your ugly thoughts or Karma will get you. Come back next week and I'll make sure you get your answers."

"Ugh! This is pointless!" I yelled and stormed away. While doing so, my shirt sleeve caught a protruding nail from her booth and ripped clean in two. Now I was wearing rags.

**I** tried hard to control my critical thoughts for the next week. Of course, the first person I ran into was Candace Smoot. I saw her walking down the hall. I willed myself not to look at her pimples and a really funny thing happened; I noticed her hair. It was glorious. It was auburn with natural caramel highlights that fell into perfect long curls. Wow. How had I missed that before?

She walked by me with her head bowed down, like she didn't want to see me or be seen by me.

"Candace," I said.

She turned to me with a look of dread. Weird. I had never said one mean thing to her.

"What?" she whispered.

"Your hair." I said.

"What about it?"

"It's really beautiful." I really meant it.

Her eyes lit up in surprise, "Really?"

"Yes, really. Don't you know it's pretty?" I asked.

"Well, my mom always tells me it is but…"

"But what?"

"I guess I didn't expect to hear it from you."

"Why not?" I asked and really wanted to know.

She got really quiet and shy, "Because you shudder every time you see me."

"Oh." I truly didn't know what else to say. "I'm sorry. That's mean."

And then she did something surprising. She smiled and said, "That's okay." Just like that. She bounced down the hall with her head held high.

**Later** that day in math, I stared at my paper completely lost. I noticed Wayne Dorrin was almost done with all the problems. I tapped him on the shoulder.

"Um, Wayne, I was wondering if you could help me with this problem? I'm kinda lost," I said.

"I won't help you cheat. Copy off someone else," he said and gave me the cold shoulder.

I tapped him again. "I don't want to cheat. I just want to learn how to do it. You seem like you're really good at math. You always get the highest grade," I said.

He puffed up a bit when I said this. "I'll help you after school. Like a tutor. There's a group of us that meet in the Media Center after school to finish homework and help each other. I won't do the problems for you, but I'll talk you through them."

"Wow, that's really nice. Thanks!" I said and meant it.

"No problem. We help some of the jocks and a few other girls too. Of course, none of them have hair as pretty as yours," he said and blushed.

That was weird. He just gave me the same compliment that I gave Candace. Is that how the Karma locket worked? I tried to make sure, but I found out that only heartfelt compliments resulted in good Karma. It was as if the locket knew when I was giving false praise.

I spent the rest of the week being mindful of my thoughts. I met the afterschool tutor club every day. Candace was one of the tutors, too. We were getting to be good friends. She actually had a great sense of humor and we laughed more than we did math. Wayne was pretty funny, too.

There were only two downsides to the

week. It was pretty obvious that Nyla and Brittnee were now BFF's. I couldn't blame Brittnee. She was a nice girl and so was Nyla. I wasn't, but I was trying hard to change that.

The other bump in the road was a girl named Eve Hunter. She was a sixth grader and pretty. I mean, really pretty. She had mocha skin and dark almond eyes. She was really smart, too. She was in pre-algebra and she helped tutor after school. She was me. Or the old me anyway. She was quick to criticize or roll her eyes. I could tell she only tutored to make us seventh graders feel inferior and in turn, to make her feel superior. I tried to keep my distance.

**Finally** Saturday came. It was the last Saturday in October and Halloween to boot. I made it through the week with only one small pimple! I had made plans to hang out with Candace and Wayne later that night. We were going to the local Haunted House.

As I approached the old lady's booth, I gasped. The most beautiful lady in the world stood in front of me. She looked a lot like the middle aged lady from last week. It had to be her daughter. She wore the same emerald nose ring as her mother and grandmother. She was breathtaking.

"I have been waiting for you," she said and smiled a dazzling white smile against her brown skin.

"I'm looking for your grandma," I said.

"Silly girl. Come and sit, "she said and pointed to a small stool next to her.

I went around the booth and sat down. She handed me a hot drink.

"This is Chai tea. It's from my country. Try it."

I sipped it. It was good! I tasted cinnamon and milk and was that nutmeg?

"Thanks, it's good," I said.

"You seem much happier than you were last week," she said.

*How would she know? She wasn't here. Her mother must have told her how upset I was last Saturday.*

"I don't mean to be rude, but I really need to speak to your grandma."

"About the locket?"

"She told you?" I asked.

"She didn't have to." She smiled like she had a secret.

"It really is a karma locket, isn't it?"

"What do you think?"

"At first, I didn't believe it. But now I do. Too many weird things have happened as a result of my actions."

"And you want to return the locket?"

"I would, but your grandma said that I couldn't."

"Yes, that is true. The locket cannot be returned. It can only be given away."

"I don't think I would want to give it away."

"Why?"

"Well, I wouldn't want anything bad to happen to the person I gave it to."

"Good answer. Then you really have had a change of heart. You could keep the locket. It may help you stay on the good path."

"Maybe. But I think I have learned my lesson."

She smiled and said, "I agree."

She got up and rummaged through a decorative box. She pulled something out that was small and flat and sat back down with a sigh.

"So now I must tell you the secret of the locket," she said, and handed me a small photograph that was the shape and size of the locket. It was a photo of me.

"Where did you get this?" I asked as goose bumps spread over my arms.

"That photograph was in the locket when it was given to me a year ago. Of course, I couldn't open it until a week ago."

"But how?" I asked

"The locket picked you," she said.

"I don't understand. I picked the locket."

"It does seem that way. But in truth, it picked you. Just as it picked me before you. It knows who needs the lesson."

I just sat there uncomprehending. She laughed. Cackled really. It sounded like her grandma.

"You were a fast learner. It took me one whole year. You said I was beautiful and that is true, but I was only beautiful on the outside. Inside I was quite ugly. I worshipped my youth and beauty. I scoffed every time I saw an old person with their wrinkles and flabby skin. Soon, I noticed my skin was becoming wrinkled and flabby, too. Only when I started seeing the true beauty each of us has inside, did the locket release me."

I shook my head, still not getting it.

"Come now. Surely you realize the old lady was me! That's what the locket did to me. And you know what? I'm grateful! I didn't know if my beauty would return. It's nice to have it back, but to be honest I was just as happy when I was old and wrinkled!"

I was shocked. I didn't know what to say.

"You're wondering what to do next?" she asked and I just nodded.

"You must pass the locket on to the next learner. But there's a catch. The person must ask for it. You cannot give it," she said.

"How will I know who it is?" I said finally finding my voice.

"The locket will tell you. Open it up."

"It won't open. I already tried."

"Try again."

I tried prying open the locket and it opened with ease. I gasped at the photo inside. Eve Hunter's beautiful face smiled back at me.

# SUPERSTITION

**My** mom quickly grabbed my hat off my bed. "What have I told you? It's bad luck to place a hat on the bed." She placed it on my head. "Especially today, of all days." She sighed.

"What? My birthday?" I asked.

"No, it's Friday…"

"My birthday." I tried to help her finish the sentence.

"No, Friday the 13th," she said looking a little nervous. "I can't believe your birthday fell on it this year. You know how I feel about superstitions."

"Yes."

We all knew how Mom was. Every little thing worried her. But I wasn't going to allow this to stop my birthday. I had planned a whole day on the water in my new little skiff by myself. I had wanted one for a while. My dad had promised me one as soon as I turned thirteen. And when I woke up this morning, I could see it from my window. It was sitting on the water tied up to the dock with a big red bow on it!

"Remember, no stupid birthday party tonight, okay?" I asked.

"Yes, you've told me a thousand times. No party. You're fishing all day. Got it." She smiled. "Can we at least have a cake?"

"Oh yeah, cake is fine. Any kind," I said. "And maybe I will catch enough fish for dinner."

"Well, that would be nice. Be careful out there."

"Oh Mom. Really?"

She just hugged me and left my room. I finished making my bed and headed to the kitchen to pack a very hearty lunch. I planned to be out there as long as I could. As I was reaching for the bananas, my dad swatted my hand.

"What the heck?" I said.

"No bananas on a boat. You know this. It's bad luck. You'll never catch any fish. How many times must I remind you about this?" he asked.

"But I like bananas. I really don't think that is going to make a difference." I threw two bananas in my backpack. As I did, I accidently knocked over the salt shaker. A few grains of salt escaped and I swiped them off the table.

"Okay, whatever." He sighed.

My dad was a semi-retired pro-fisherman and I had heard this banana theory my whole life. He told me stories about how if someone brought a banana on board their boat during a tournament, they would throw the guys whole lunch into the water.

My mom walked in the kitchen just in time to notice the overturned salt shaker.

"Who spilled salt?" she said and grabbed the shaker. She shook some salt over her left shoulder.

Wow! I didn't realize how superstitious my parents were. I wondered if my little sister did. I started whistling as I headed outside.

"No whistling in the house," my mom yelled at me. "It invites the devil inside."

I didn't stop whistling. This family was getting a little crazy.

"Hey, sis?"

"What?" She was busy reading a book on the lounge chair on our porch and didn't even take her eyes off the page.

"Are you superstitious?" I asked.

She closed her book. "I don't think so, why?"

"Because Mom and Dad are driving me crazy. Every little thing I do today is supposedly bringing bad luck." I sighed.

"Well, it is Friday the 13$^{th}$," she said.

"So, what?"

"So, if there was ever a time to be superstitious, it would be today."

"Not you too," I said. Sometimes reading too much isn't a good thing. Ha!

I noticed a ladder beside the porch. That's right; Dad was supposed to work on the gutters today. I thought I would have a little fun with my sis. "Oh no, look! I'm walking underneath the ladder," I said loudly enough for her to look. She did.

"Why would you do that? Really Michael, now you're just asking for it."

I crossed under it one more time just to make her mad.

"Hey, I just realized that your name starts with an "M" and it is the thirteenth letter of the alphabet," she yelled out to me.

I was already down by the dock and just waved my hand like I couldn't hear her, even though I really could. Ebony, the neighbor's cat, ran by me fast. She looked like a blur. That was weird; a black cat crossed my path. Wait a minute, what was I thinking? Who cares? That didn't mean anything.

I threw my backpack in the skiff and untied it from the dock. I jumped in and started the motor. Well, tried to start the motor anyway. My new boat was not co-operating with me. I saw a few luminous clouds starting to appear. Noooo! Not today. I wanted to have a fun day by myself on the water. Maybe catch a few fish for dinner.

Luckily, I had oars inside the boat just in case something happened to the motor. I tried the motor one last time. It worked. I headed out onto the water. Even with the clouds overhead the water was serene. I found a peaceful spot and turned off the motor. I expertly baited my hook and threw my line in the water. I felt my shoulders begin to relax. I guess all that superstition stuff got to me more than I realized.

Being on the water always calmed me. I guess I got so relaxed I fell asleep. I didn't wake up until the raindrops hit my face. They were big and fat. Not a harsh rain but a very slow and steady sprinkle. There was only one huge raincloud, so I knew that it was only temporary. I checked my line, nothing. Bummer.

A loud splash made me turn my head. I swear I saw a fishtail. It was enormous. It had scales on it; beautiful scales that flashed iridescent.

*And was that a giggle I just heard? Where did that come from? I was surrounded by water. Did I just catch a glimpse of long red hair under the water?*

I shook my head to clear my thoughts as images of beautiful mermaids swam through my brain. The rain stopped as quickly as it started.

I felt something bump under my skiff. Fish! I put a fresh fat worm on my hook and plopped it in the water. I got a nibble instantly. I instinctively yanked up on my rod to set the hook in the fish's mouth. I was rewarded with a nice, fat bass.

I removed the hook and tossed the fish into my bucket. I baited my hook again and started the process all over. After fifteen minutes, I was rewarded with four plump bass. Perfect for dinner tonight.

As I was getting ready to head for home, the skies opened up. It rained harder than I've ever seen it rain before. My little skiff started filling up with water. I tried to start the motor, but it wouldn't catch. I began paddling frantically to get back to the shore.

I knew what I had to do; I just didn't want to do it. Finally, I dumped the four plump bass back into the lake and began bailing the water out with my fish bucket. As soon as I did this, the storm abated.

Somewhere in the distance I could have sworn I heard a girlish giggle. I'm positive I spied another flash of red hair and an iridescent tail. A mermaid? Surely not! Although they were known to tease fishermen. And hadn't I just got the biggest tease ever with four great fish that I had to throw overboard? This was becoming a jinxed day after all.

As I was nearing the dock, the only good thought I had was at least there would be cake. I kinda wished my family was throwing me a party. It would put me in a better mood. Could all this have happened because I was purposely tempting fate by mocking old superstitions?

I tied up my skiff and headed up to the house. My arms were sore from all that paddling and I was drenched to the core. I couldn't wait to get inside to warm up and ask my dad about mermaids.

There weren't any lights on at the house. That was very unusual. I entered through the front door and flicked on the light switch. No lights. The storm must have knocked the power out.

"Hey everyone, I'm home!" I yelled. I was ready for this day to end. I knew if I could just hear a "Hey buddy!" from my dad that this strange feeling would go away. But no one answered.

I felt a cold chill creep up my spine as I walked through the kitchen and into the living room. There I saw a sight that I will never forget.

Even in the darkness, I could see both my parents lying on the floor. They were completely covered in blood! No! Their bodies looked twisted and contorted. My mother's head was lying across my father's chest. I was getting ready to run upstairs to check on my sister when I saw her emerge from the kitchen.

She was carrying a birthday cake aflame

with thirteen candles. She had blood dripping from a gash in her neck. She was walking slowly like she was in a trance.

"Happy Birthday," she whispered. "I wish you would have heeded our warnings about superstitions. Look what you have done." A sneer spread across her face.

Just then my parents stood up and moved towards me like zombies.

"Yessss," my dad hissed. "You should have lissstened."

"Always lisssten to your mother," my zombie mother added.

I was getting ready to sprint for the door when the laughter started.

My family started laughing. My dad went over to the lamp, screwed the light bulb in tight and turned it on.

Stupid me. I can't believe I fell for it!

"Boy, we got you good!" my dad laughed.

"We sure did," my mom added. "Sorry, honey. It was too easy with your birthday falling on Friday the 13th and you not believing in superstitions."

"I don't think I've ever seen you that scared." My sister giggled as she placed the chocolate cake on the table.

"Very funny," I mumbled.

"Blow out the candles and make a wish," my mom said.

I already got a great present; my skiff. And I have a fun family that knew how to play a practical joke. *What could I wish for?*

Just then, the image of a red haired beauty flashed in my mind. I blew out the candles and could have sworn I heard a fish splash in the lake, followed by a girlish giggle.

# AUNT MARGI

**I** sat next to my big brother in the back seat of our sedan. I was dressed in my Sunday finest, as were my brother and mom and dad. My mom looked worried as my dad steered our old Sedan through the neighborhoods of our home town.

My Great, Great Aunt Margi had passed away and we were on our way to her funeral. My mom said we had to stop by her house to retrieve some paperwork her lawyer needed. As we pulled up to the house, I shivered. I never liked that house. It was creepy. My mother sent my brother in to pick up the papers. He went reluctantly. He didn't like the house either.

You could tell that an old person had lived in the house for a very long time. The shrubs and trees were overgrown. Her fence sprouted honeysuckle vines and their wily nature gave her front yard an ominous look. A big magnolia tree dropped brown leaves that littered her walkway.

The house itself wasn't much better. It was made of stone and was probably an adorable cottage in its youth, but now it was just a rundown eyesore. My brother and I always hated going over to visit Aunt Margi. Unfortunately, my mom insisted on monthly visits. She said it was our duty as the younger generation. Since Aunt Margi was too old to come to us, we had to go to her.

We had two options during these visits. If the weather was foul, then us kids were relegated to the kitchen; but most days we were told to play outside. Aunt Margi was old school and believed that children did not, under any circumstances, belong in the living room when adults were visiting. So outside we went.

But as I mentioned before, outside was creepy. Aunt Margi's yard was so overgrown we were afraid to play in it. We tried once and ended up with poison ivy. That was enough to convince our young minds that the house was indeed, out to get us.

The house had a carport that was full of junk. In the corner stood a rusty old lawnmower that had seen better days. My brother told me that the lawnmower was possessed and could come to life at a moment's notice. He said it came to life a couple of years ago and it chopped off Aunt Margi's toes. I believed him whole heartedly because she was, in fact, missing her toes off her right foot. So, with this information at hand, we made up a game to see who could get closest to the lawnmower before it came to life and attacked us. It was scary and thrilling at the same time. My brother somehow always won. He didn't seem as scared of it as I was. It wasn't until I was an adult that I realized Aunt Margi had lost her toes due to poor circulation. My brother made the lawnmower story up to scare me.

It was mean to think, but I was grateful that we didn't have to visit Aunt Margi anymore. I hated how you had to kowtow to her when you were at her house. Like, if you had to go to the bathroom while you were there, you had to run by the creepy lawnmower and into the side door that led to the kitchen. You crossed the hallway and stood in the doorway to the living room. You asked for permission there; never daring to enter the living room. Heaven help you if you did! Not even a child's small toe was allowed in her pristine living room. Aunt Margi was a funny old gal and kept her house spotless on the inside while the outside slowly decayed. She even had the plastic coverings still on her furniture! Even still, the whole house smelled musty like an old lady. Gross.

One time, I scraped my knee and hobbled into the living room to get my mom's attention. Aunt Margi yelled at the top of her lungs, "Get out of my living room!"

My mom carried me to the kitchen to soothe my minor wound.

Scary old lady. I would not miss her. As I was thinking these thoughts, I watched the front door of the house for my brother to return with the papers. Suddenly, he flew from the house and jumped into the car. He was white as a sheet as he slammed the car door shut.

"What happened? Are you alright?" My dad asked concerned.

"Not now," was all he said as he glanced at me.

My dad drove away without another

word. Later I saw my brother whispering to my mom and dad in the corner at the funeral. I was scared and wasn't about to ask my brother what happened. I am pretty sure he wouldn't have told me anyway. He was pretty scared and that made me scared. My brother was tough, and I'd never seen him frightened of anything.

Several years went by and I had forgotten about Aunt Margi. That is, until one fall evening when my brother and I were sitting by a crackling fire and looking through some old photos of days gone by. There was a picture of Aunt Margi sitting on her couch in her living room, looking stern and unsmiling. As I held the photo, I thought back to the day of her funeral.

"Remember how mean Aunt Margi was?" I asked.

"Yeah, she really hated kids, didn't she?" he answered.

"I always wondered what happened to you on the way to her funeral. What did you see?"

"Do you really want to know?" he asked.

"I think I can handle it now," I answered.

"Well, Mom sent me in to get some papers. Unfortunately, they were located on an end table in the living room. As I entered the house, it was dark because the power had been turned off. I felt my way through the hallway and into the living room. A small sliver of light shone through the curtains, spotlighting the stack of papers. As I picked up the papers, Aunt Margi's ghost appeared sitting on the couch. Her face screwed up into a scowl and she yelled in a voice like a demon, 'Get out of my living room!'"

"My God," was all I said.

I looked down at the photo of Aunt Margi sitting there on her couch, smiling proudly. I could have sworn she was scowling in the photo just a minute ago. I flicked the photo into the fireplace as an act of primal self-preservation. A draft from the chimney flue carried the smell of a musty old house to my nose as the photo crackled and burned.

# SLAYER

**I'd** never thought my powers were that special, but I guess to a normal person they would seem quite extraordinary. That is if a normal person even knew about them. I can communicate with animals. I know it sounds fun and generally it is, but there are times when it's a curse. And this was one of those times.

I never really liked Halloween; too many creatures come out of the darkness. Now when I say I can communicate with animals, that also includes mythical creatures beyond imagination. And those creatures only venture out on Halloween.

The sun was going down and I was getting ready to arm myself for the night's festivities. I told my parents I had a babysitting job. They never questioned me as I'm a good kid; I always made the honor roll and had lots of friends that they liked.

I opened my backpack and I threw in my belt of three horns, my elven dagger, the flute of Rosina, eye shades, a bandana, iron stakes, my favorite leather gloves, a torch and a lighter. I was now prepared.

I don't know how these creatures knew where to find me, but they always did. I have been attacked by them for the last five years. And the attacks are getting harder and harder to fend off. I have had to do intensive research on how to protect myself from them. The local librarian thinks I'm really into mythology. She seems to find out things I can't even find online. She doesn't realize I'm actually living the mythology or does she?

"Don't forget to turn off the outside light when you leave, honey. I don't want Trick or Treaters stopping here," my mom yelled to me.

"Okay," I turned off the porch light. I often wondered why my parents didn't have the powers I had. Maybe it skips a couple of generations.

As I walked into the night sky, my mind

was alive and my body was ready for action. Sometimes these creatures appeared as soon as I got outside, other times they'd wait for me to summon them. Either way, it was going to be a long night. I headed over to the middle school's football field. It seemed to be a portal for these mythical ones. *Who would have thought my school a portal?* Very surreal; eerie silence and not one creature in sight.

I reached into my backpack and took out my belt. It held three horns. I wrapped it around my waist. I attached my dagger to my leg. I could feel its strength against my thigh. I placed the torch and lighter close down by my feet.

I grabbed the first horn of my belt. It was the largest of the horns. I raised it to my lips. I blew as hard as I could. One long blast and two short ones. No sound came out, but I knew that it was doing its job. Only the Hydra could hear the inaudible tone. The Hydra was a horrible, multi-headed beast that could kill you with its breath and poisonous blood. I hated those snakelike heads.

I could see the Hydra approaching me through a swampy area next to the school. I tied the bandana around my neck. The Hydra wouldn't be the fastest creature tonight, but it was one of the trickiest because when one head would die, two would grow back in its place.

I started counting heads before it reached me. Right now there were six. So potentially, there could be twelve or more if I wasn't careful.

I lit the torch and held it in my left hand. I pulled the bandana up and around my nose and mouth. I unsheathed my dagger and held it in my right hand. I was ready for battle!

The Hydra made the first move. It lunged at me with one of its heads and tried to breathe on me. Luckily, my bandana protected me from its nasty breath. I swiped at its head and managed to cut it off. However, I wasn't fast enough with my torch and wasn't able to burn the stump where the head was a second ago. Because my reaction was too slow, two heads sprouted up from that stump.

Hydra blood dripped from the tip of my dagger. I wiped it on the grass. The grass withered and died. Hydra blood was so poisonous that if it touched your skin you would be paralyzed for two minutes giving the Hydra plenty of time to finish you off.

Seven snake heads laughed at me and that made me angry. I approached it with my dagger high. In two quick slashes, I cut off the two new heads and burned the stumps with my torch. The laughing stopped. I continued my battle until all the heads were cut off and all the stumps were burned.

The Hydra slithered off into the darkness. I was drenched in sweat. I wiped my brow with my bandana and then used the bandana to wipe my dagger clean. I threw the bandana on the ground. It disintegrated in less than thirty seconds.

There was no time for rest, for I knew that my name was being cursed in the mythical realm because of my first slaughter tonight. As soon as I caught my breath, I heard a far off howl. It sent shivers down my spine. It could only be the black dog or hell hound, as the horror movies called it. It was invisible to humans, except for the ones it hunted.

I could see the red, demon eyes in the distance. This one was coming for me! Parts of its fur were on fire. Staying alert was the only option at this point. If its prey looked in its eyes three times, they would die. That was how powerful they were. If they didn't stare you down, their elongated, pointed fangs could rip you in two. The black dog was running straight for me.

I put on my leather gloves and placed my eyeshades high on my head. I wasn't ready to use them yet, but I needed them on my head for easy access. I was nervous. No, I was scared. The closer the creature got to me, the bigger it seemed. Its paws were enormous. It was as big as a cow if not bigger.

I grabbed the second horn and emptied the contents around me in a circle. The salt made an impressive ring of defense. That would buy me some time; about three minutes if the librarian was correct. The creature stopped in its tracks. It couldn't penetrate the circle of salt. Thank goodness! I put some iron stakes in my pocket.

The creature kept circling around me trying to get me to look in its eyes. I accidently did look directly in its eyes for one second. I could feel them burning instantly. I looked away. I had to watch myself; I wasn't ready to die. I reached for the last horn. I blew with all my might.

In a flash, I was invisible. I only had thirty seconds before it wore off, and the creature could see me. I jumped on its back. It couldn't see me, but it could feel me.

The creature tried to shake me. A couple of times I was barely holding on and I looked in its eyes for the second time. I quickly put the eyeshades on. I couldn't see, but at least I was protected.

I stabbed the creature in the side with one of the iron stakes. It didn't stop it at all. I stabbed it again with another stake. This time the creature started slowing down. The third stake did its job. It went stiff and unconscious. This was the moment I was hoping for. I put my hands around its thick neck and squeezed as hard as I could. I couldn't feel a heartbeat. I felt around some more until it was pulsing in my hands. The fur was hot, almost on fire. Even through the leather gloves I could feel the heat. I pushed on its lifeline until the pulsing stopped. It was dead.

The creature disappeared underneath me, and I fell to the ground. I took off my eyeshades and sat cross-legged on the turf. It took a while to catch my breath.

The battle was over for the night; for the year, actually. I was physically and mentally worn out. I was ready to head home. There was only one thing left for me to do. I put all my weaponry back in my backpack and took out the Flute of Rosina. I played the melody as I had done for the last five years. Within minutes I saw the crow flying over my head. It circled around my head five times and dropped a scroll from its talons. I caught it, and the crow disappeared quickly.

I took a deep breath and slowly opened it. Only two words were scribbled on it. BASILISK and CHIMAERA. Those would be the mythical creatures I would have to fight next Halloween. I had no idea what they were. I guess I will be heading back to the library tomorrow. At least I would have a whole year to prepare. Happy Halloween to me!

# SECRET

**I've** always been a curious person, even when I was a toddler. I guess a girl gets like that when she grows up without a father. My mother never mentions anything about him, so I always seem to be making up my own stories in my head about who he was.

"The only thing you ever need to know about your father is that his name was Godric Vladd Gravemore, and that's final!" My mother would argue.

"A twelve year old girl deserves to know more than that about her father!" I would shout in reply.

Whenever I tried to talk about him, she changed the subject. I never thought much of it; I just brushed it off and pretended like it never happened. Until today.

My mother had another twelve hour shift at work, so I was all alone in our big house. I got bored from playing games on my Wii, so I decided to go on my own adventure around the house. My room was the castle, since I'm the princess of the land. The basement was the dungeon because it's always been musty. The office was the village market. The guest bedroom was the horse's stables. And Mother's room was the mysterious village that my castle was going to take over. If Mother found out that I was in her room, I would be totally grounded! She says I'm never allowed to go in there.

Since there are no rules in my village, I went right for her room. I was amazed at how boring it was. It made me wonder why I was forbidden to ever go in there in the first place. The walls were plain white and didn't have a single pretty design on them. The flooring was made of beaten up wood. She had a small and firm bed. The comforter was the only interesting thing about her room. It was red with a little black cat on the bottom corner. That didn't seem like my mother at all!

I was anxious to explore the rest, so I went

right into her bathroom. That's where things got weird. It was huge! It was as big as two of my rooms put together. The concrete walls were so old that the blocks were crumbling apart. Her bathtub was a big black hot tub: very eerie like a cauldron! Misshapen, dusty, leather books filled a makeshift bookcase. In the center of the bookcase was a wooden box with a big keyhole in the middle.

*What could she be hiding in there?* I asked myself as I examined the box. My curiosity got the best of me and I began to fidget with the box. It wouldn't open.

I knew I needed to find the key if I wanted to open it. I searched all over her room, but to no avail. I even tried my house key, but the hole was much too big for an average key.

The key I was looking for was the size of a small book. And then it hit me! I ran back to her bathroom and I took apart all of the books. They were really odd books, too: *Broomsticks N' Things, Spells for the Dead, Witch's Guide to Cover a Murder*. Then I found a book that was pretty torn up that had the initials G.V.G. written on the cover in black, cursive ink. Those were my father's initials! I threw open the book as fast as I could. The inside had only one page. It was crinkly and had a yellow tint. It simply read "The key to unlock the box to Godric Vladd Gravemore."

I had no idea what that meant, so I flipped the page. The book was hollowed out and held a giant gray key with blue and purple stripes. It had one big loop at the top, followed by a smaller loop right under it. It looked like an old fashioned skeleton key. I was amazed by the beauty of it. I ran my hands over its smooth, cool texture. I was so absorbed with it, I almost forgot what I was doing in the first place. When the key fell out and hit the hard wooden floor, I remembered my mission and got back to work.

I picked the key up and inserted it into the box. I jiggled it and sure enough, it fit! I clicked it to the right and felt the lid pop up. I cautiously opened the lid, but nothing could have prepared me for what I saw. I found the skull of a man inside the box. Just as I reached to pick it up, I felt a strong tap on my shoulder. I jumped around to find my mother standing right in front of me. She held a wand in her right hand and a broomstick in her other.

I started to scream, but she quickly put her wand to my lips. Before I knew it, a bright, white flash flowed out of her wand and coiled into a slip that covered my mouth, sealing my lips shut! I tried to push her back, but she did the same to my arms. I was tied to the wall.

She stood there looking at me for a few seconds and then finally spoke, "I knew that this day would come, Rowan. I'm guessing by now you know that I'm not like most mothers."

*Obviously not. What mother keeps her true identity from her daughter?*

"When you were born, your father discovered that I wasn't such a good witch. He tried to take you away from me and have me locked away forever. It was a fight to the death, and it didn't end so well for him. I put a spell on him that only you could unlock with that key. And now that you have done so, you must die!"

I was frozen in disbelief. I couldn't do anything to stop my mother! I was frozen there, unable to speak or fend for myself. I knew that this would be the end for me. Mother grabbed her wand then slowly raised it to my face. I could taste the saltiness of my sweat dripping down my face onto my lips. That's when I knew that I couldn't go down without a fight.

My arms were bound, but my legs were free. My mother was close, so I jumped up and kicked her. She stumbled back and bumped into the box that held my father's skull. His skull crashed to the ground.

Just then, a cloud of green dust spewed out of his skull. I watched in astonishment as the skull started to sprout almond colored hair. Skin started to cover the newly formed bones. Emerald eyes popped open in a flash. Grotesque little nubs expanded into muscular arms and legs. The final product was a very handsome man. He wore a black cloak with a hood and a rigid wand.

I was standing in the same room as my father!

Without hesitation, he waved his wand and I was freed. He sprang in front of me to block me from my mother's vicious attack. The deadly, enchanted rays from her wand ricocheted off my father and hit her instead. My mother fell to the floor, gasping for air.

**"Rowan!** Help me!" my mother pleaded as she was drowning in the wand's rays.

I looked at her with sorrow in my eyes, but I knew what had to be done. My mother was nothing but an evil old witch who had intended to kill me. Still, I was upset. I turned away and ran into my father's arms. He hugged me while my mother slowly died.

When the screams stopped, I looked back and saw her robe and wand surrounded by a pile of ashes. I turned back around, but no one was behind me. My father was nowhere to be found. There was only a glass vial with a sheet of paper attached to it. I picked it up and read it aloud to myself.

*Rowan,*

*I hope that you now understand that your mother was a good witch gone bad. You're strong enough to go on without her. This vial holds your own powers. Use them for good. I can't be with you right now, but you will see me soon.*

*~G.V.G*

I choked back tears as I set the note down and held up the vial. I popped open the corkscrew that held the magical dust. Beams of blue and purple sparkles shot out like fireworks. It sprinkled around my body and I felt a rush flow through me.

When it stopped, I felt strange, but strong. I opened my arms and a black cloak fell into them. In the cloak was my own wand; emerald, just like my father's eyes. I didn't know what I was meant to do next. All I knew was that I needed to learn how to use and control my powers.

I packed a few things in a small bag and walked out of my house; never looking back.

# ANGEL

I had just scored the best babysitting job any fourteen year old girl could ask for. It was the Friday before Halloween and a lady my mom worked with asked if she knew any teenagers who would be interested in sitting for her two year old. My mom volunteered me, which was fine after I heard how much the lady was willing to pay.

My mom dropped me off at the house around six o'clock later that evening.

"I'm working a short shift at the factory. I'll pick you up around midnight when I get off," my mom said and waved at her friend who had just come to the door. She was a pretty lady in her thirties.

"Hi, I'm Joelle Campton. Come on in," she said.

"Thanks," I said.

"I'll give you a quick tour."

She led me into a beautiful two story house. You could tell it was old, but it had been well cared for.

"Your house is really pretty," I said as we walked into a huge kitchen. It smelled wonderful, like cookies.

"Thanks. This was the house I grew up in. I just moved back home with my family after my mom passed away."

"Oh, I'm sorry."

"It's okay. I miss her terribly, but I'm grateful she left us the house. Would you like a cookie?" she said. She held out an old fashioned cookie jar that was shaped like a cat. I greedily took a cookie.

It was heavenly, crunchy on the outside and gooey chocolate on the inside. "It's really good," I mumbled with a full mouth.

Joelle laughed. "I know. It's my mom's recipe. She always had a way of taking care of everything. Somehow she knew just what was needed in every situation. Now come upstairs and meet my daughter, Bridgett."

Bridgett was a pretty little girl with fair hair and big eyes. She was already in her jammies, snuggled in bed. Her daddy was reading a picture book to her.

"You're just in time to finish the story," he said.

Bridgett pulled the covers up over her head, nervous to meet a new person.

"I'd love to read a story," I said. "But I think I need help from my friend, Mr. Squirrel," I said as I pulled a squirrel puppet out of my bag. I had read all the books on babysitting and picked up a few tricks. It worked like a charm. The Campton's were off after a few final instructions, and then Bridgett and I were alone.

Two more stories told by "Mr. Squirrel," and Bridgett was sleeping soundly. I crept downstairs and helped myself to a small plate of chocolate chip cookies and a glass of cold milk. I walked into the family room and turned on the TV. A reporter on the local news was covering a story about a disturbed man who had escaped from the local home for mentally ill people. He was considered dangerous. I turned the channel immediately so I wouldn't get freaked out. A documentary about ghosts was on. They were talking about how ghosts communicated with the living.

I decided to see what my friends were up

to online. I logged onto the Internet and chatted a while. Everyone was talking about what they were going to wear to tomorrow night's costume party.

Suddenly, a message popped up on my screen. It said, "Did you lock the front door?" and it was signed by someone calling themselves, *Angel*.

I was instantly creeped out. I didn't know who Angel was and then I realized it was probably one of my friends trying to scare me. They all knew I was babysitting because I had just updated my Facebook status.

"Very funny," I typed back, but not before I checked the front door. It wasn't locked. I locked the doorknob and the deadbolt.

Back in the family room, I nibbled on another cookie and watched the ghost show. Now they were talking about how ghosts could call people on the phone. That was stretching it a bit, I thought.

Another message popped onto my screen.

"Did you lock the windows?" was signed again, *Angel*.

"Very funny! I get it. Scare the babysitter close to Halloween. Ha-ha," I typed back. But I did check the windows, every window on both floors. Two were unlocked on the first floor.

I was a little more than scared, but I didn't want to admit it. I knew I could call my mom if I got really freaked out, but then she might think I wasn't ready to be a proper babysitter. And I really liked the idea of making some money.

"What about the basement? Is it secure?" *Angel* typed.

"Not funny anymore!" I typed back.

I was so paranoid now that I knew I had to check the basement if I wanted to get any peace. I turned on the lights leading down the stairs and started down. It smelled damp and a bit moldy. I jumped about a foot when my head hit a cobweb. I debated again whether or not to call my mom.

The basement door was locked, but one of the windows was not. I locked it and ran back up the stairs, taking them two at a time.

I checked on Bridgett. She was sleeping soundly. I headed downstairs and decided to play some games on my computer to distract myself. I played for a good hour and finally relaxed. I drifted off to sleep on the couch and awoke to the sound of the front door knob rattling. I thought it was Bridgett's parents returning home, but then the rattling stopped. My computer gave off the instant message sound, but I ignored it because I thought I heard someone jiggling the front window.

The instant message sounded again. I ignored it again because I was sure I heard another window jiggle.

I began to reach for my phone when the instant message sounded again. I glanced at my computer screen and saw the same message flashing three times; "TURN ON THE OUTSIDE LIGHT! TURN ON THE OUTSIDE LIGHT! TURN ON THE OUT-SIDE LIGHT! *ANGEL*".

I flew to the front door and switched the front porch light on. It flooded the lawn. I saw a big scary man turn and look at the house. He looked startled and a little crazy. He just stood there like he didn't know what to do.

I grabbed my phone to dial 911, but stopped in mid-dial because I heard police sirens in the distance.

The police cars flew around the corner and two police men jumped out. From the front window, I saw them tackle the man and handcuff him! After the police had him in the squad car, they came up to the porch and knocked on the door.

"Yes?" I answered with wobbly knees.

"We just wanted to make sure everyone in here was okay."

"We're all fine here," I answered, willing my voice not to shake.

"It's a good thing you turned the porch light on. I don't know if we would have seen him in the dark. We've been looking for him ever since he escaped from the mental institution earlier tonight."

I assured the officers we were fine just as my mom and the Campton's pulled into the driveway. After lots of hugs and reassureances, Joelle invited us in for a glass of hot cider to calm our nerves.

We sat around the table sipping cider and talking about the mysterious messages I had received, which seemed to warn me about the mad man. I laughed it off as if it didn't really scare me, because I didn't want to lose a good babysitting job.

"I'm sure it was just one of my friends joking around, but I'm glad they did it." I laughed nervously. "I just wish I knew who it was. They signed each message as *Angel*. I guess I'll never know."

"I know who it was," Joelle Compton

said.

"You do?" I asked, wondering how she could possibly know any of my friends.

"Yes, I do. It was a person who always knew just what to do in every situation. You see, Angel was my mother. Angela was her full name, but everyone called her Angel because she always made sure everyone was safe and sound. She was looking out for you and Bridgett tonight."

"That's not possible. Ghosts can't send messages through the Internet." I said, but then I thought, *or can they?*

# ABOUT THE AUTHORS

This book was written by the Nardini Sisters. Lisa Nardini, is the oldest sister, Gina is the middle sister, and Sucia is the youngest sister. Marina Ummel is Sucia's daughter. They all live in Florida, except Gina, who lives in North Carolina.

The Nardini Sisters come from a family of story tellers: their dad, Ben, their Uncle Geno, and their Aunt Sarah. They all could spin a yarn that would keep you on the edge of your seat!

Visit their website at:
www.nardinisisters.com

Can't get enough of the Nardini Sisters? Check out these other titles available at www.amazon.com.

## The Underwear Dare
## Nerd vs. Bully!

Eddie's the biggest, meanest bully in Ms. Waverly's fifth grade class and Josh is his favorite victim. So when Josh's dad marries Eddie's mom, things go from bad to worse. Escaping the bully is no longer possible now that they share a bedroom.

When Josh's dad announces that the attic will be turned into a bedroom, Josh is thrilled. But who will get the room? The decision is left up to the boys. The boys concoct a series of disgusting and embarrassing dares to decide the fate of the prized room.

*Read only if you can handle being grossed-out by popping vomit, silent but deadly farts, vibrating burps, and other dares not for the faint of heart!*

# Zoo'd
## 6th Graders vs. Primates!

Josh and Eddie are at it again when an overnight field trip to the zoo goes awry. As newly appointed Junior Zookeepers, Josh, Eddie and pals find themselves solely responsible for the well-being of the animals after a huge storm knocks out all power and communications. The gang becomes locked in a battle of wits with the Colonel, a militant monkey who has escaped during the storm. As the Colonel and his mini-monkey army wreak havoc, Josh and Eddie plot to catch them. Will the boys triumph or will they be made monkeys of?

*Read only if you can handle crazy poo-slinging monkeys, giant sandwiches, zip-line adventure, and exploding bubble gum.*

Coming Soon:
Camp-Off! A Josh and Eddie Adventure!

Made in the USA
Lexington, KY
30 August 2015